BROUGHT TO LIGHT

ELIOT GRAYSON

Cover by Stephanie Westerik

SMOKING
TEACUP
BOOKS

Published by Smoking Teacup Books
Los Angeles, California

ISBN: 9798394397424

For everyone trying to get the job done with inadequate, insufficient,

or just plain confusing resources.

Chapter One

Callum

Parking didn't pose a challenge in this sleepy little northern California beach town, but I pulled into a spot a block down from my destination anyway. Better to keep a low profile.

My mark's place of employment, the Chipper Bean, was the only business on the block with a light on. (Stupid fucking name, and if I'd been going after whoever came up with it, I'd have been a lot happier.) The sign offended me as much as the name, featuring a grinning coffee bean with very large, very white teeth and a pair of aviator sunglasses. The bean clutched a steaming mug, presumably full of coffee.

Had Cannibal Bean already been taken when they named the place? Either way, the logo looked goddamn happy to be swilling the juices of its fellows. I scowled at it and pulled the door open, setting off a cheery jingle.

One customer hunched over a table by the front window, wearing headphones and staring at his laptop. Another stood at the register ordering, next to a counter with a glass-fronted section holding some sad-looking pastries and another counter with cream and sugar. A few other scattered tables sat empty.

And working away at the espresso machine, wreathed in a

cloud of steam, was the guy I'd been sent here to kill.

Not even a guy, really. A *kid*. He'd looked goddamn young in the photo, but in person he could've been a high-school student. He stood maybe less than an inch shorter than my own six-feet-even, so not small in that sense, but a stiff breeze could've sent him floating away like dandelion fluff.

His hair, which drifted around his face in a cloud of white-blond waves, didn't really help; it made him look even more like a dandelion, and even more fragile.

I got in line behind the guy at the counter. "Be right with you," my target said brightly, his voice as light and sweet as his looks.

Well, this was just fucking great. My mood took a final plummet, ending up somewhere underneath the artfully scuffed floorboards. The kid—John, according to the file I'd memorized, and I'd never seen anyone who looked less like someone named plain John—had a wide fucking smile. Rosy lips. White, slightly crooked teeth.

And as far as I knew, he'd only made my hit list because he existed and someone out there didn't like it. They hadn't even offered the justification of making bad coffee.

The barely veiled threats had been very much present and accounted for, though. They knew who I was. They knew who my handler was. They knew everyone we'd ever been in contact with. And they'd made it clear that if we didn't do what they wanted, they'd decide they didn't like *us* existing, either.

Fuck. This.

John gave the customer his drink along with another megawatt grin and turned his attention to me. I felt like his brilliant blue gaze should've been an X-ray, showing every flaw down to my murderous bones. But he kept smiling.

"What can I get you? I make a great hot chocolate. It's a little late for coffee, although—maybe you like to stay up all night?"

His smile dimmed just the tiniest bit as I scowled at him, and he blinked. Was he fucking *hitting on me*? Not that I didn't swing that way sometimes, but Jesus. This kid didn't have one single ounce of self-preservation hidden anywhere on that willowy body. I'd picked my bulky leather jacket on purpose to hide my weapons and also conceal the lines of my own body. I was well-built. Years in the army and a few more years of doing what I did after the army had made me that way. But I tried to play it down, blend in a little. I didn't look hot like this, not even from the neck down. I looked stocky, and big, and unshaven, and probably only about a tenth as dangerous as I really was—already ten times more dangerous than anyone like John should've been getting anywhere near.

"Hot chocolate sounds good." I wasn't going to drink it, anyway, so what did it matter?

He winked at me. Actually *winked*. "It's a good thing you chose wisely, because I'm going to make sure you try it and tell me if you like it!"

I nodded at him, dumbfounded, and watched as he spun gracefully on his heel and started steaming a pitcher of milk. I wasn't really the kind of guy to go with the flow. Usually I was the one who stopped whatever the flow was, often permanently.

But apparently I'd be drinking hot chocolate.

And then, after that, I'd find a place to lurk, follow this kid home, and figure out the best place and time to kill him and make it look like some kind of freak accident. In a town this size, a mugging wasn't all that likely. And my blackmailers—sorry, clients, whoever they were—had been deathly fucking serious about not attracting attention or causing a big police investigation, a real challenge when you left a dead body behind.

Maybe I'd make the body disappear; make him disappear. Fake some kind of note to his friends or roommates about running off to Thailand to find himself. His file said he didn't have any family. Maybe no one would ever bother to look for him. I'd be the only one to know for certain what happened to that pretty smile and those bright blue eyes, to know where that slender body lay rotting away. The keeper of his final secrets.

A paper cup with a mound of whipped cream materialized in front of me. I looked up sharply, realizing how long I'd been staring down at the counter and completely ignoring my target and my surroundings.

John wore another sweet smile, this time with a bright, mischievous look in those sparkling eyes. "You seem like you're secretly a whipped cream kind of guy," he said quietly, as if we were co-conspirators.

I hadn't thrown up in years, but it took every bit of willpower I had not to lose what was left of my late lunch.

"Yeah, sure," I said hoarsely, but I couldn't bring myself to pick up the cup. "What do I owe you?"

"Three-fifty!" He poked the cash register and stood there expectantly. Was his hair actually floating around his head, or was that an optical illusion? If I hadn't known better, I'd have thought a gentle spring breeze had drifted by, making his soft waves flutter.

God, I was fucking losing it. I pulled out my wallet and gave him a five. "Put the change in the jar."

And then I had to get out of there. I picked up the cup, even though I wished I could run away and leave it.

"Try it?" he asked, his tone barely shy of pleading. "Just a taste. Let me know what you think. I'm sort of new at this. I need feedback."

According to the file he'd been working here for months. If he didn't know how to make a fucking hot chocolate by now, he had to be hopeless. And hadn't he said he was great at it?

Still. I put the cup to my mouth, and then hesitated. Jesus. It held cocoa, for fuck's sake. Not rat poison.

Probably. But I knew what rat poison tasted like. I'd be able to tell.

I took a sip, having to slurp the whipped cream to get to the liquid under it.

My eyes widened. It was…the best thing I'd ever put in my mouth. Without question, without any doubt, it tasted better than the first beer after basic training, or the lips of the first girl I'd ever kissed in tenth grade. It was fucking ambrosia.

John's eyes were fixed on me, oddly intent. "You like it?"

"It's amazing," tumbled out of my mouth before I could stop it. "It's good. Really, really good."

Until his whole body relaxed, I hadn't noticed John's tension. He carried himself so lightly that it hadn't been obvious. But he seemed to settle, his whole posture looser. Jesus. Was he afraid of losing his job if someone told his manager he made shitty hot chocolate? Was his manager the same person who'd chosen the sign out front? If so, maybe I'd make another stop on my rounds.

"Good," he said. "That's—good. Thanks for coming into the Chipper Bean!"

I managed a growl that could have been words, turned, and hightailed it the fuck out of there. Maybe I'd go back after an hour and follow John home; maybe I wouldn't. It could wait another night. Fuck.

Hot chocolate in hand, I wandered down the street. I really wasn't in the mood for strolling casually through the picturesque downtown of a shabby seaside tourist trap, gawking at the fishing-themed this and driftwood that and shell-encrusted whatevers. Fuck that.

And my mood itself pissed me off even more, because the day *after* a job was almost always the worst. Not that I usually regretted what I'd done, or got worked up all that easily, but the adrenaline took a bit to wear off. A lot of preparation and careful planning went into my jobs, and executing that plan—shitty pun intended—always put me in a heightened state of awareness that took time to fade away and left me with a wicked hangover.

First approaches, though. They tended to give me a high: the thrill of the hunt, the beginning of something new. But this day-before-a-job felt like all the days after I'd finished rolled into one, with a heavy, nasty sensation in my gut and a snappish irritability that I just couldn't shake.

The sidewalks were fairly empty. On a Tuesday night, in the middle of January, no one wanted to be out in the chill—coastal northern California was surprisingly cold for a state with a reputation for sun-drenched beaches. No one was shopping; they'd already returned all their crappy Christmas presents and gone to ground to stare blankly at the screens of their new electronics.

Fuck them, too.

I headed down the street again until buildings gave way to scrubby grass dotted with wind-bent trees, all spreading out until it merged with the beach. I stared out over the Pacific, or what little of it I could make out between the darkness, the overcast, and the fog underneath that. I wasn't really seeing it anyway.

The hot chocolate warmed me from the inside in a way that didn't have much to do with its temperature. I thought of John, his sweet smiles and the grace in his long limbs. What the fuck had he done to bring death down on himself? You never knew. I'd killed a guy one time who looked like a kind old grandfather, gave massive amounts of money to animal charities, fostered abandoned kittens, and financed a bloody rebellion in a small South American country that had ended with the deaths of thousands of civilians.

But John hadn't armed any revolutionaries, and he didn't have a past. I'd checked, or rather, my handler Jesse had checked. Jesse dotted every *i* and crossed every *t*. And Jesse said the kid didn't have a past, didn't have any skeletons, and that we had to kill him anyway because we were dead men if we didn't.

Fuck, that was good hot chocolate. I drained the last drop, tilting the cup up as far as it would go, and barely restrained myself from licking the inside of it. Killing someone who could make something taste that amazing had to be a crime…okay, yes, killing anyone was technically a crime. But not a crime I gave a damn about most days.

I crumpled the cup in my hand.

A second later I had my phone out, and Jesse answered on the first ring, sounding a little breathless, like he expected me to be mid-emergency.

Well, wouldn't be the first time.

"Tell me again who those assholes were," I said without any preamble or pleasantries.

"If I knew who the assholes were, I'd be researching how to get them off our backs, wouldn't I?" he snapped. Jesse valued the pleasantries. God only knew how he put up with me. "No ID, but they knew the right names to drop and the right hints to make. We've been over this. Callum, they were *someone*. You think I can't recognize spooks? These motherfuckers had those *eyes*, you know?"

I did know, but I rolled mine anyway, glad he couldn't see me and give me shit for it. Jesse could be so fucking dramatic.

"Okay," I said. "I believe you." Which I did—and I also needed to cut him off at the pass before he got all poetic. "But there's something really fucking off about this. The whole thing reeks. I made contact tonight, and in person...fuck, Jesse. You didn't see this guy. He's not—the usual."

Not that we exactly had a usual in our line of work, but older, richer, and creepier were a lot more common.

Jesse sighed, a whoosh down the line that made me picture him puffing up his cheeks and glaring. "I know he's not," he said quietly. "But nothing about what we do is usual. Make something up about him. Some backstory that'll let you live with this. But—it's him or us, Callum. It's up to you. I can't do it for you, and I wouldn't be able to anyway. But that's the trade-off here."

I ended the call just as confused and wired and pissed as before, only now with extra guilt on top. Jesse couldn't do the job for me. That wasn't his part of the deal. But if I didn't go through with it, he'd pay the price right along with me.

Because I did believe him when he said the two assholes

who'd shown up on his doorstep were the real deal. Jesse had been Air Force Intelligence before an explosion ended his career early and sent him home with about ninety percent of the body he'd started with. He wasn't an idiot, and he wasn't inexperienced.

I stuffed the phone into my pocket and walked further down the beach, staring out at the gray nothingness of the foggy ocean until my eyes burned. I kept coming back to the million-dollar question: why me? Why hire a mid-grade freelancer for a job when they could've easily done it themselves?

So if it was a setup, somehow—and I really, really had trouble picturing anything else—what did I gain by doing the job? I'd be getting fucked either way, I was pretty sure. So: kill the kid, get fucked, hate myself? Or leave the kid alone, get fucked, and know someone else would only kill him later anyway? The first option had a very slightly higher chance of getting me and Jesse out alive.

Was it worth it, though?

Fuck. I had to do it tonight if I meant to do it at all. The more I thought about it, the less I'd have the stomach for it.

With new determination, I strode up the beach and back toward town, ignoring the sharp, persistent feeling of wrongness that tightened my gut and stiffened my neck.

A few stragglers were trickling back to their cars and heading home for the night. I passed a stoned-looking guy sitting and dozing against the side of a darkened bait and tackle store, a young couple holding hands and eating ice cream despite the drizzly weather…and then my eyes caught and held. A block ahead of me walked a dude almost sketchy enough to be someone I'd know, wearing a battered brown leather jacket in the same weapon-concealing style as my black one and with shoulders almost broader than mine, too. He shot a quick glance over his shoulder from under bushy brows, and I instinctively sidestepped, flattening myself against the side of a building.

I crouched down and adjusted the laces on my boots, turning sideways so I could keep an eye on him and so that I'd be less likely to attract his attention if he noticed me…and putting myself in a good position to pull either of my guns quickly, too.

Because let's be real, he'd recognize me, even without knowing me, the way I'd recognized him. Everything about this guy pinged my radar; he was another me, I'd have sworn to it. And it strained any credulity I still had left after the life I'd led—almost zero, in other words—trying to imagine there could be two assassination targets in this one small town.

He'd come here for John, same as I had.

He turned at the corner and went on his way without a second glance behind him. Cool as a cucumber, the motherfucker. He had to have clocked me in return, and if the possibility of getting shot in the back concerned him at all, he didn't show it.

I stood up and licked my lips, tasting the salt of the ocean fog and a hint of chocolate and whipped cream. Double fucking fuck. The Cannibal Bean would be closing right now, John locking the doors and going about his business, mopping and putting things away, completely unaware that outside the little bubble of the café there were two ruthless killers hunting him like prey.

If I didn't kill him, my opposite number would.

And if that asshole got to John before I did, Jesse and I would be in what passed for breach of contract in my line of work. Put another way, we'd be next up for a bullet to the back of the head.

Little as I liked it, I had no choice.

Gametime.

Chapter Two

Linden

After a few months of repetition, closing up the shop had become automatic: shut the door and flip the sign, clean the espresso machine, wash the dishes, count the register, sweep and mop. Restock all the little things on the coffee bar. And so on and so forth.

That particular night, it was really lucky it had become such second nature, because I couldn't have focused on work to save my life. The glaring overhead lights, so different from the lamplight and candlelight of my home, were giving me a headache, and the strange, prickling, pressurized sensation in the air didn't help. It felt like it might've before a thunderstorm. But while the skies had been overcast earlier, they hadn't heralded that kind of weather.

It wasn't from the weather. It was something else.

My mind kept circling back to the customer from earlier in the evening, the big one, the obviously dangerous one, who stuck out in this small, sleepy town like a wolf in a flock of stoned sheep. I'd been warned not to use any magic while hiding out here. When Lady Lisandra, my mother's employer, had told me to run, she'd made it clear that I had to live a human life. Magic could be sensed, could be traced; it would be a beacon for any of our people who crossed over to hunt me. I wasn't powerfully magical, but the inability to use what little I had made me feel itchy in my own skin. Vulnerable, and off-kilter, and even more isolated, since magic was at the moment my only link to my home.

So using it when I made his drink had been self-indulgent in the extreme, and dangerous to boot. But I'd had to know if the man meant to kill me. After all, what would be the point of hiding if I'd already been found? Yes, our laws prevented us from doing one another harm while in the human realm. Direct harm. Harm that could be proved in one of our high courts.

But it would be very, very difficult to prove that my death by human means had been orchestrated by one of our own. We couldn't lie, which meant we'd spent untold thousands of years honing our prevarication, omission, and evasion skills to a degree humans would be unable to differentiate from lying.

The man had felt like a killer, from his wary stance to his prowling gait to the way his eyes took everything in, cold and hard and observant. He repelled me nearly as much as he drew me in, pushing and pulling on my instincts with his intensity. Fear, after all, caused responses in the body nearly indistinguishable from powerful attraction. Men like that were best avoided, but what was best for me wasn't always what I wanted. And he had such strength, such confidence and surety in every movement and even in the timbre of his voice. Half of me had wanted to drop my pitcher of milk and run, never looking back. The other half had wished I could leap over the counter and beg him to stand between me and anyone else who might want to hurt me. To give me at least the illusion of safety in this strange, foreign place.

I'd had to know which of my instincts to follow. So I'd put a trickle of magic into his drink. And it had tasted good to him.

He couldn't possibly mean me any harm—if the magic didn't lie.

Fae magic, like fae lips, *couldn't* lie. But it could prevaricate, omit, and evade. It answered any question you asked, but it never,

ever prompted you to change your question if you'd chosen the wrong one in the first place.

So I brooded, grinding coffee beans for the morning and setting the coffee carafes upside down to dry and seeing only that man's harsh face, the look in his dark eyes as he'd tasted what I'd made for him. Should I run again? Where would I go? I could go home. Sick anxiety pooled in my stomach along with the latte I'd made myself right before closing. I didn't want to die. I didn't want anyone I loved to die. I was so alone here, and if I died here, it would be without even the comfort of knowing I was mourned.

I put the night's take in the safe along with the register float and shut and locked it. So close to being done here for the night, and then I'd have to really face the decision in front of me. I couldn't go home. My mother would be in more danger if I did, along with Lady Lisandra and her entire household. Lady Lisandra's nobility didn't include importance. Nor enough influence to defend herself against a sorcerer with an army of fanatical followers—a man who'd worked himself up into a paranoid frenzy about the blatherings of a senile seer, interpreting them to mean that I was the one destined to end his life.

Lord Evalt had clearly lost the plot. I was a cook's bastard son, little better than a peasant. I possessed no wealth and no title. My magic was mediocre, my skills with weapons nonexistent. I made excellent hot chocolate, even when I didn't enchant it, and spectacular hot chocolate when I did.

Unless Lord Evalt suffered from a lethal milk allergy, I didn't pose much of a threat to him.

And yet here I was, cowering in fear for my life in a place where I knew no one and was at least as vulnerable as I'd have been at home.

Which brought me right back to the danger I'd put others in if they tried to protect me, and also right back around to the front of the shop, where I just had to put the chairs back down off the tables before I'd be ready to leave.

My apartment was only a few blocks away from the Chipper Bean, but I didn't think I could stand to go back there to be locked in all night, terrified of what might lurk outside the flimsy door and windows. I'd go mad, pacing and brooding and also wondering what was wrong with me. After all, the only person who'd sparked a flicker of interest since I came to this town was possibly a psychopath and also possibly, hot chocolate test aside, planning to kill me.

I flipped off the lights, locked up behind me, and turned to face the empty street. No one. Not even the old man who often walked up and down this street in the evening "getting his steps in," as he'd told me. I took a deep, shuddering breath, redolent of salty fog, delicious and clean, and set off toward the beach, mind made up about my destination, at least. I had to clear my head, and one thing I truly detested about the human world was the lack of fresh air in heavily inhabited parts of it. Standing in the breeze off the ocean, closing my eyes and letting it ruffle my hair, I could pretend I'd never left home, and that when I turned I'd be standing on the cliffs near Lady Lisandra's manor, looking down over the rolling, wildflower-speckled green hills to one side and the turquoise waves to the other.

I stopped at the corner, wishing the diner was open so that I'd have somewhere to go. Somewhere safe, with people around. And they had the best pancakes I'd ever had.

Not that I had extensive knowledge of pancakes. We didn't make pancakes back home. But I loved them. I'd made a mental note to bring my mother a recipe if I ever got to go back and spend a peaceful morning in the kitchen with her. Those mornings had seemed so bloody boring when I'd had an endless number of them; now I'd have traded centuries of my life to have that back.

Across the street and one more block down, I reached the end of the row of dinky shops and dusty law offices and weathered bicycle racks—and stopped dead in my tracks.

A man stood at the end of the street, right where the

pavement started to blend into the beach, with tiny dunes heaping the edge of it where the wind had blown the sand every which way. He didn't have the height or the broad shoulders of the one who'd been in the shop earlier, and what I could make out of his face in the light of the nearest streetlamp didn't look attractive at all—but he'd been cut from the same dangerous cloth. It stood out all over him. He was a killer.

And his glinting eyes were focused on me.

I wavered, like a deer trying to decide which direction to run from a wolf. The man grinned, baring his teeth.

Oh, fucking bloody fuck. His very sharp teeth, the ends pointed like they were all canines.

He didn't belong to this world.

I spun, broke, and ran like every Tarkunian demon chased me, snapping at the back of my neck. I didn't dare look behind me, but I could feel him approaching, the weight of his eagerness for my blood nearly palpable against my vulnerable back.

Where had everyone gone? Where was the man who walked up and down, the diner's nighttime janitors, the evening dog-walkers, people who'd see him and scream and call the police and frighten him away? Or perhaps he'd only kill them all to get to me…I ran and ran, my feet pounding a frantic tattoo on the side-walk, my heart skittering along in a counterpoint rhythm that felt like it might burst my rib cage.

My arms pinwheeling, I careened around the next corner, hoping to find some cover, somehow—and an arm came out of nowhere, catching me right across the stomach and sending me flying. I landed on the ground hard enough to bruise my arm and side and knock the wind out of me.

I rolled to my back just in time to see the man from the night before, a gun in his hand. My attacker rounded the corner and launched himself at me, crying out in a language I recognized as one of my own world's.

Were they going to kill me together? In sequence? Would I be more dead that way?

But I wouldn't go down without a struggle, no matter how useless it would be to try to fight either of them.

Callum

Not gonna lie, my instincts were screaming at me to do the one thing I knew I wouldn't have to think about, agonize over, or worry about: follow the son of a bitch right that second and cut his throat.

But I didn't. Because I wanted to, and I wanted to because it was so much goddamn easier than going and doing the job I'd actually been hired to do.

So I forced myself to think it through from the perspective of someone who hadn't suddenly gone soft. If I followed my opposite number, I'd run the risk of causing a scene that'd blow my cover as someone who wasn't in town to cause murder and mayhem. John would run, and Jesse and I would be fucked even if I caught up with him later. If I went after John immediately, I ran the even more serious risk of Asshole Two (I was number one, of course; I might be honest enough to take the title, but I'd damn sure be the one on top) sneaking up behind me and killing both of us.

Which left me with one viable option: waiting for Asshole Two to go after John, and then sneaking up behind him and killing them both.

He wouldn't do the job in the middle of the street if he was a professional, which he had to be if he'd been brought into this the same way I had. The interested parties who'd approached Jesse had made it damn clear they didn't want a fuss. Which meant he'd either lurk near the Cannibal Bean or he'd head for John's address and wait for him there. My best bet would be to find a position that gave me a view of the entrance of the coffee shop in case that was the chosen venue. From there, I could discreetly follow John home.

Carefully circling the block to make sure I didn't have company and that I wouldn't be followed in turn, I eventually installed myself behind a dumpster near the mouth of an alley across the street from the Cannibal Bean.

And then I loosened my main weapon in its holster under my arm and leaned up against the wall to get comfortable.

John would be closing up in about fifteen minutes, and then he'd need to do all the stuff diligent retail employees did at the end of the day. Fuck if I knew; I'd worked in a grocery store for about five minutes when I was in high school before I got fired for punching a dude who hit on the girl collecting the carts. But it had to take half an hour or so, I figured. Either way, I had some time to kill. So to speak.

Not that I had anything I wanted to think about.

The seconds dragged by, then minutes. Finally the lights went out in the coffee shop and John emerged and locked the door behind him. If he went home—and it wasn't like this town had any night life, so he didn't have much choice—he'd turn right and pass me on the other side of the street.

For a moment he simply stood there, pale face turned up to the sky, eyes closed. How did his skin glow like that without any moonlight or anything? No one looked like that under a fluorescent streetlight.

Turned out he did have a choice, because he opened his eyes, shook his head, and turned left, walking briskly the way I'd gone when I went down to the beach.

Oh, fuck no. If I hadn't been in stalking mode, I'd have kicked something. He'd be easy prey there. No one around, the sound of the waves to cover anything—I couldn't be sure the other guy wasn't watching too, no matter how carefully I'd checked. He could've circled back after I did, for one thing. John had a head start. If I ran after him my footsteps would give me away. If I'd simply waited on the beach myself—fuck.

So I did the only thing I could do. I spun and jogged down

the alley away from the main street. I'd run parallel, catch up with them on the dunes, and pray the killer didn't get the job done and disappear to report in that I *hadn't* gotten the job done before I could take him out too.

Someone had to die tonight, but it wasn't fucking going to be me.

Chapter Three

Callum

At the end of the block, a noise made me pause. Fuck, the sound of pounding feet. Two sets, and getting closer. The other guy might've been ahead of me, but he'd flushed our quarry out and sent him right back into my waiting arms. I flattened myself against the side of the brick building on the corner and had my Beretta in hand within a millisecond. Closer, and the sound of panting breaths—and then John, his hair flying wildly and his face pink and shiny, barreled around the corner.

I shot my arm out and caught him around the waist, neatly clotheslining him and sending him sprawling on the ground.

John let out a cry of surprise and pain and rolled onto his back, just in time for the other set of pounding feet to close in.

An instant later, Asshole Two came around the corner and launched himself at John, snarling something in a guttural language I couldn't understand, his—Jesus Christ, sharpened—teeth gleaming.

Sometimes, when I was in a situation like this, time slowed down. Became elastic. Every detail struck me at once, but I processed them individually: John's wide, panicked blue eyes, sheened with tears, maybe; the flash of something in the other guy's hand, a knife with a wickedly curved blade; the damp of mist or possibly the start of rain cooling my cheeks and settling in my hair; the weight of my gun in my hand.

John was my mark, a dead man the second Jesse told me we had to take the job. That was how it worked. There simply couldn't be room for anything else.

I flipped the gun in my hand, grasping it neatly by the barrel, and time sped up again. John cried out, raising his bruised and gritty palms to fend off his attacker, and the grip of my pistol thwacked into the asshole's temple with a meaty crunch. He collapsed like I'd cut his strings, his face smacking into the pavement and his limp arm falling across John's legs. The knife gleamed against the dull concrete, reflecting the pearl-gray of the sky like a mirror. It looked—the knife was a single bone, sharpened to a point at the end. The fuck. No matter how useful a spare knife might be, I wouldn't be touching that fucking thing.

Something else fell out of his other hand and rolled onto the sidewalk: a plastic flashlight, it looked like. Without thinking too hard, I snatched that up and stuffed it in my pocket. I didn't have one, and I might need it later. Digging graves went easier if you could see what you were doing.

John stared up at me, his pink lips parted, giving me a glimpse of his teeth. His tongue flicked out to wet his lower lip. "Is he dead?"

I shrugged. "Probably. Or will be, if no one gets him to a hospital." I hadn't flipped the gun around out of any desire to spare his life. I just hadn't wanted the noise of a gunshot to attract attention.

John suddenly scrambled out from under the dead weight of the guy I'd maybe just killed, rolling to his knees and panting heavily, his head hanging between his shoulders like he was trying not to throw up.

Fucking civilians. I caught him around the upper arm and hauled him to his feet. He was as light as he looked. Dandelion fluff. His hair brushed my chin as he lurched upward, and a shiver went down my neck.

My fingers went all the way around his arm. I gave him a squeeze, and not a gentle one. He shuddered.

"Who the fuck is this, and what did he want?"

Of course, I already knew the answer. But I needed to know if he did. I still had no idea why the spooks wanted this kid dead...but John might know. And what he knew might save my life, or Jesse's, if this went even further fucking south.

"I have no idea what his name is," John said, his voice wavering. "I was on my way to work. He—tried to kill me."

All my bullshit alarms started to clang. I'd fully expected an answer like that, and I'd even been prepared to possibly believe it.

But John *did* know, or he had some idea, anyway. John knew he was a target. And that made the total innocuous emptiness of his file sound like a part of the setup—even though Jesse's research hadn't turned up anything more. The quaver in his voice, the way he couldn't quite look me in the eye, the fidget of his hand—it all told me he was lying. And not that well.

I tightened my grip, hard, drawing out a yelp of pain, and yanked him around to face me. We were chest to chest, and I glared him right in the eye. He was just that tiniest little bit shorter than me. It was enough. I knew how to loom.

"You know who the fuck he is," I growled at him. "And you're going to tell me."

His eyes widened impossibly more, turning into big blue innocent pools that were perfect for an idiot like me to fall and drown in.

"I—I swear," he stammered. "I don't know his name."

Who the fuck cared about his name? "Why was he trying to kill you? You know what, fuck that," I said. He was just standing there in my grip, pliant and passive, and it was pissing me the fuck off. And a rapidly dying body lay on the ground two feet from us. It was plain fucking luck no one had come down the street yet.

Quiet as it was, we were in the middle of town. "We're finishing this somewhere else."

I flipped my gun around and tucked it into my jacket pocket, with my hand still wrapped around the grip, my finger loosely alongside the trigger guard, and my thumb over the safety. I wouldn't be able to shoot John by accident, but I could draw my weapon or even fire through the jacket in half a second. Sketchy, knifey, and probably dead might have friends. Or competitors. For all I knew, the client had opened the job up for a bidding war.

Another narrow alley ran behind the building I'd been pressed up against, lined with a couple of battered trash bins and a heap of rotting plywood. I dragged John along it at double-time, mentally mapping out where to go next. The logical thing would be to get out of town, somewhere deserted, and leave John's body buried in the sand where it wouldn't turn up for a while. Or better yet, weight him down and drop him in the ocean, maybe off a small cliff where the water was deeper.

John stumbled along next to me, somehow managing to be light and graceful in his movements even when they were jerky and uncoordinated. How the fuck that worked, I didn't know.

"What's your name?" I demanded.

I didn't expect an answer. "Linden," he said after a beat, and it startled me enough that my head swiveled so I could stare him down.

"Linden."

He glared at me in turn, looking more stubborn than I'd thought a face that unnaturally pretty could be. "Yes. I'm not lying." He let out a little huff of a laugh.

"Hell of a name to make up, anyway," I muttered. Wasn't a linden a type of tree? Whatever. I didn't know a damn thing about trees, except that they made good things to hide behind when someone shot at you.

Speaking of which. We'd reached the other end of the alley. I pressed John—Linden—up against the wall, trying to ignore the warm give of his body against mine. Talk about stuck between a rock and hard place, the poor little fucker. A dirty brick wall on one side, and the man sent to kill him on the other.

I peered out around the corner. One way led back to the downtown area. A guy walking his dog crossed the street at the intersection. Fuck. He was heading the way we'd come from. He'd stumble over the no-name assassin in about thirty seconds. In the other direction, a car was coming, a plain blue Volvo station wagon with a wild-haired hippie dude at the wheel. Hopefully he was fully baked and wouldn't even remember us, but either way, I didn't have a choice.

I slid my hand down Linden's arm and grasped his wrist, turning my arm so that it might kind of seem like we were holding hands if you weren't looking too closely. "Casual," I hissed at him, and sauntered around the corner and down the street.

The Volvo passed us without pausing. I started to move a little faster, counting down in my head. The guy with the dog…we were less than a block away when I heard barking and a shout of alarm, right on schedule.

I sped up again, tugging Linden along, knowing he could keep up, what with how long his legs were. They were longer than mine, even though he wasn't quite as tall. Long, and slim, in those stupid fucking skinny jeans.

He did keep up, striding beside me without even trying to get away.

And why would he, right? I'd rescued him. He was a naïve kid. I'd killed the guy trying to hurt him.

Except that no one could be aware they were being hunted and not be suspicious of a guy with a gun who turned up out of nowhere, right? How was he not terrified?

I glanced at him sidelong. I could see the whites of his eyes, framed by ridiculously long blond lashes. His lips were parted, and his breath came in shallow little gasps.

All right, he was terrified. But he wasn't trying to get away.

Maybe he had a lot more brains than I'd given him credit for, and instead of taking me at some *Thank God this dangerous man turned up to save me* face value, he'd already worked out that I had my gun pointed at him, and he had no chance. He could scream and try to bolt, and I'd shoot him and run. Or he could go with me and hope to get an opportunity later on, or maybe talk me out of it.

That wasn't fucking happening. I'd repeat that to myself as many times as necessary, because right then the thought of blood soaking that fine silky hair and staining it crimson made me sick to my stomach.

At the end of the small row of buildings along the street, town became country again and the street we'd been on turned into a rural road. It led inland, winding through a lot of scrubby trees. No time to cross over to the ocean side of town. We had to get out. More distant shouts echoed behind us. The dog walker had attracted some attention, apparently.

I pulled Linden across the road, trotted up a small hill, and then put on a burst of speed, sliding down toward a creek lined by tall trees with branches stretching out as if they wanted to grab us with leaves as their reaching fingers. The leaves rustled, too, a low susurrus that sounded like a chorus of whispering voices.

They didn't sound friendly. Fuck. Where the hell had that thought come from? I hadn't been myself all evening, not since that hot chocolate. Jesus fucking Christ, had he slipped something into it? But I could worry about that later.

I skidded to a stop on the muddy bank of the creek and flung Linden up against one of the trees, taking a couple of quick steps back as he sprawled against the trunk. It was gloomy as hell under the trees, what with the lack of moonlight to begin with, but I could still make him out, his face and body almost…glowing? The fuck. He really had drugged me. But if he had, he wasn't happy about the results, because his pale face looked ashen gray, and his lips were white.

"Don't fucking move."

I pulled the gun and thumbed off the safety, slipping my finger around the trigger, pointing it right at his midsection. Linden nodded jerkily, his fingers curling against the tree behind him.

Warning Jesse had to be next now that I had a hand free, because in a situation like this, minutes were the difference between life and death. He had a plan for this, I knew that; I just didn't know exactly what that plan was, a safety precaution to make sure I couldn't be tortured or drugged into betraying him. I pulled my phone out of my pocket with my left hand, opened a new message and—hesitated. Was this worth throwing away everything we'd built up, worth forcing Jesse to abandon his life completely?

Yeah, yeah it was. The presence of another hitman on the scene meant we were truly fucked. The client didn't trust us, and wanted to tie up loose ends. We were dead men if we didn't run, even if I finished the job—and we might be dead men anyway if we did run.

Forgot to check the oven, I typed quickly. *Turn it off*.

Next I'd need to tear the phone apart and make sure it couldn't be traced, but…what the fuck was that sound? The whispering had risen in both volume and intensity, and the leaves…the leaves were shaking. There wasn't any wind. And the leaves writhed like snakes over our heads.

"What the fuck?"

I looked at Linden. He didn't seem surprised. And his mouth was moving, silently, but somehow I knew his lips were tracing the same sounds the trees were making. I opened my own mouth to say something else, to demand answers—answers to what, though? What the fuck was the question, even?—when the sound built to a shout, a shout made entirely of hissing and rustling and the roar of wind through branches, even though there *was* no wind.

The tree behind Linden shivered and shuddered, and its trunk grew and faded all at once, graying out into an expanding mist.

Linden slid backward, falling into it, being absorbed within it.

The phone fell from my hand, and I lunged, seizing a handful of Linden's T-shirt and holding on with all my strength as he pulled away from me. The shirt tore, and I dived after him, wrapping my arm around his waist and falling with him, the mist swallowing us both.

Chapter Four

Callum

A dripping sound, and then a faint whispering echo. I forced my eyes open. Nothing. I blinked, and still nothing.

I was alive. I was lying on something cold and hard.

Had I gone blind, or was it truly pitch-black? The complete absence of light was rare, unless you were underground.

Dripping sounds, a faint whispering echo, cold and pitch-black…yeah, okay, the signs all pointed to underground.

I levered myself up into a sitting position, and something hard pressed against my hip.

The flashlight I'd taken from Asshole Two, and I took a second to thank past me for having at least a tiny bit of foresight, even if I'd fucked up everything else today. I pulled it out and clicked the button, keeping my gun aimed in the same direction. A faint, feeble blue beam stuttered out. In the absolute blackness of wherever the fuck I was, it definitely helped…but it wouldn't go far enough to give me warning of a potential danger. Maybe the batteries were loose. I clicked it off and unscrewed the end of it, sticking my fingers in to press them down.

Except there weren't any batteries. The flashlight was empty.

I clicked the button again, and it turned on.

The sensation of being high that'd been building for a while only increased. Talking trees. That fucker's sharp teeth and that bone knife, like nothing I'd ever seen—and I'd seen, and stabbed and been stabbed with, a lot of knives in my time. And now…

What the fuck had been in that hot chocolate? I'd taken acid, and shrooms, and my share of other weird shit over the years, but none of those hallucinations had ever been this real. This tangible. Okay, so I hadn't slept much the night before. But I'd gone without sleep for longer than that before and still functioned just fine in a war zone, so hanging around a rural fucking town in California shouldn't have been an issue.

Of course, I might not be in California anymore.

Fuck. This was what I got for waiting to kill Linden, for trying to have a fucking conscience for once.

And for thinking someone that pretty couldn't hurt me. I knew better than that.

Fuck it. No matter what had happened, how I'd gotten here, it didn't actually make a difference to my next steps. All of this might be in my head. I could be in a coma somewhere. But I had no choice but to deal with the "reality" I could see and touch and taste.

So I shone the flashlight around, keeping the Beretta aimed with it. But there wasn't much to see, and definitely nothing I'd want to touch or taste. I had damp, filthy stone under me, something like flagstones, only not quite as even. The wall across from me looked like the same stuff. I turned my head. The wall behind me, ditto. I played the beam in the other two directions. I was in some kind of hallway, not a room, and the light didn't go far enough to show me more than stone floors disappearing into the darkness both ways.

The ceiling, when I turned the flashlight up, was more of the same, only with some darker patches of moisture. I'd halfway been expecting the *Alien* queen, since that was what you got for looking up last, but I couldn't even see a spider. The ceiling wasn't too low, probably eight feet. That'd get claustrophobic after a while, but at least I wouldn't need to crouch.

I saw no sign of Linden.

Well, fuck.

I stood up, cracked my neck, shook out my limbs, and leaned down again to examine the floor more closely. I went about ten feet to my left, using my original orientation as a starting point. One of the flagstones glowed faintly, with a light blue symbol in the middle of it. Nothing I recognized, of fucking course. I shook my head. Maybe it meant something I couldn't begin to interpret, and maybe I'd finally gone crazy enough that glowing stones were par for the course. Anyway, I doubted Linden had stopped to write on the floor with glow-in-the-dark sidewalk chalk, so it wasn't relevant at the moment. I headed back the other direction, examining the floor the same way.

And there it was: one single golden pointy leaf, muddy and crushed, no doubt stuck to Linden's shoe when we...did whatever we'd done. And wasn't that a mind fuck, but at the moment that went in the low-priority column with the rest of the weirdness. Whatever had happened, I wasn't about to be able to reverse it. Wherever I'd landed, I was stuck, and I had no option but following Linden.

Because he'd done this, somehow, or at least known enough to let it happen. He was my way out. Or if not my way out, then my only source of answers.

And fuck it, but he was still my mark, and I was fucked if he'd get away via magical melting tree, of all the stupid fucking things.

I could smell him, I realized as I moved noiselessly down the hallway after him. A faint, fresh scent of green things and running water and under that, a hint of coffee and chocolate and spice. I kept getting a whiff of it, easy to distinguish from the musty damp of this place.

Even though I'd intended to destroy my phone, I wished like

hell I still had it. Yeah, the GPS could be used to track me, but better tracked than hopelessly lost. Google Maps seemed like they belonged in another universe from this place. And my phone's flashlight would've been ten times more useful than this hallucinatory piece of shit.

My time sense was pretty good, and it felt like a little more than an hour before I came to anything different: a branch in the passageway, a T-intersection, with tunnels going to the left and right. I scouted down both directions, but I couldn't smell anything different, didn't see any more leaves, and couldn't find so much as a trace of Linden. There were more glowing squiggles on a few of the stones, but I'd passed quite a few others along the way, too. I hadn't been able to discern any pattern.

Fuck. I hesitated in the intersection, taking a minute to evaluate my situation overall.

The tunnels had plenty of air. Maybe it smelled like mildew and dust, but it wasn't stuffy. That meant there were outlets—somewhere. I didn't have any food or water, but weirdly enough, I didn't feel thirsty or hungry yet. That was a good sign. I'd spent eighteen hours wounded behind enemy lines in Afghanistan once without any supplies, and I'd been fine. I could handle this for at least a couple of days.

I had the flashlight, which didn't show any signs of flagging any more than its lame baseline level. It wasn't like the nonexistent batteries were going to run out, after all.

Fifty-fifty. Linden had gone one way or the other. Given my luck lately, I wasn't sure I liked those odds.

I had a knife in one of my boots, so I pulled it out and marked the wall with an arrow pointing toward the intersection from the direction I'd come from. I could keep doing that; as long as I never passed an arrow pointing the wrong way, I couldn't go back and forth along the same tunnels like an idiot. Theoretically I could've used the glowing symbols to remember where I'd been, but some of them repeated, and they all looked more or less the same anyway.

I hesitated a little longer. This kind of indecision wasn't normal for me. I'd only stayed alive because I'd gotten so good at making decisions quickly, usually under fire. But the idea of getting out of here, and never knowing what had happened to Linden…it didn't sit well with me. If he disappeared here, wherever we were, well—technically my job was done.

But if the job got done, it'd be because I'd taken care of it myself, damn it. Letting it get done by default felt *wrong*. As if, dead or alive, he was my responsibility. And stupid feelings aside, he might still be the key to figuring out who'd wanted him dead in the first place. Jesse was out there somewhere, on the run. I'd be on the run as soon as I had somewhere to run to other than these tunnels. If either of us wanted to live any kind of life once this was over, I needed to use Linden for any information he could provide.

I stood perfectly still and listened, even clicking off the flashlight to give my other senses a chance to compensate. A very distant dripping sound. The faint rush of my own calm breaths.

And then a jagged, horrible scream.

It echoed up and down the tunnels, but it had come from—my left. Definitely my left.

I clicked the flashlight back on and double-timed it down the passage, hoping I wouldn't hit another junction, since I couldn't stop to mark the wall.

Because that scream wasn't the sort of thing you put off checking on. That was terror and pain, and I'd heard enough of both to know.

The timbre of it made me almost certain it was Linden. My heart didn't pick up, because it never did. But my jaw clenched, and I had to fight a wave of something like fear of my own.

My boots smacked the stone, sending cascading echoes ahead of and behind me. Whoever was fucking with Linden, they'd hear me coming, but I didn't have a choice. Another scream rang out as I ran, and I put on a fresh burst of speed. I heard something else, too, a weird growling and—slapping? Like a wet towel on concrete. It was unsettling as hell. All the hair on my arms rose, like when you were the prey, not the predator.

Fuck that. This place might be fucked-up and foreign, but that was my normal. And I was the predator everywhere.

The passage ended in another T-junction, but the growling and Linden's cries were easy to follow, and I swung right and was on top of them.

Some—thing—had Linden pinned against the wall. He was fighting it like a madman, but he was losing. Its jaws snapped right next to his neck, its long arms almost had his pinned, and it scrabbled at him with its clawed feet, trying to gut him like a cat with a rodent.

Even though it had four limbs, its greenish, shiny, slimy surface made it look less human than even the conspiracy theorists' little gray alien men.

The thing spun its head, showing me glistening flat-white eyes and a mouthful of curved, serrated teeth, and I lifted my hand and put a bullet right in the middle of its forehead. The impact rocked it backward, but the bullet went straight through and cracked against the wall. The deafening report of the gun hit my eardrums like a giant fist. Linden flinched, and the creature's grip loosened. I lunged forward and caught it by the neck, my fingers sinking in like I'd grabbed a handful of Jell-O. Fuck, it was disgusting, and I flung it as far from me as I could. It hit the ground with a wet splat and didn't move.

For a second no one moved. Linden panted, staring at me with wide eyes, a shadowy figure in the edge of my flashlight's weak beam. I had the light trained on the thing I'd shot, and my gun trained on its chest, ready to put another few rounds into it— or through it, as the case might be—if it so much as twitched. Slowly, carefully, I got close enough to nudge it with my foot. No reaction.

It didn't seem to have any bones, or a skull at least, but

apparently a nine-millimeter round directly through the head killed just about anything, thank fuck.

"It's dead," Linden said, his voice hoarse.

I kept my eyes on the thing. The longer I examined it, the more bizarre it got. It looked like it was deflating, almost, like it really was made out of gelatin and only sheer willpower had kept it up and moving around. The gooey eye sockets seemed to be seeping into the eyes the longer it lay there. Its eyes weren't white anymore. I would've really liked to look away, but I needed to give it another minute. Tempting to put a few more rounds through it on principle, but I had no idea where we were, how long we'd be here, and what else might be hanging around. I wasn't going to waste ammunition I might need later.

"You know what this is?"

"Not—exactly," Linden hedged. He cleared his throat. In my peripheral vision, he straightened up, wincing a little and patting himself down as if checking out the damage. "I knew there were things like this. But I've never seen one before."

"Yeah? Well, that puts you miles ahead of what I know." I finally stopped staring at the fucked-up oozing thing on the floor. It'd flattened out almost completely, and it was obvious that what-ever 'alive' meant for it, that was over. I turned to Linden in time to catch another wince. Good. He ought to feel a little guilty.

Linden looked at me almost pleadingly, his eyes round. And maybe that would've worked if we were in a bar and he'd been trying to get laid, but right then, standing over the corpse of some monster out of a nightmare that I hadn't even known could've been trying to kill me as I wandered through this Godforsaken labyrinth, it just pissed me off.

"There's no way for me to explain any of this without making myself sound crazy, in the context of what you consider normal. I know this is so far outside of anything you can understand—I mean, there's no way to—"

I holstered my gun and lunged, and he squeaked as my hand

wrapped around his throat and pinned him to the wall. I leaned in, our faces only inches apart. Because that was enough condescending bullshit on top of the fuckery sandwich that had been my day.

"*Normal* flew out the fucking window when some pointy-toothed motherfucker carrying a trick flashlight tried to gut me with a bone," I growled at him. "And speaking of teeth and bones, *normal* isn't things with teeth but no bones running around in fucking stone tunnels that we got to by going through a melting fog tree, *Linden*." I squeezed harder to punctuate my point, and he let out a startled little *eeep* as his hands flew up to tug on mine. I hardly felt it. "So I don't need you trying to help me explain away reality, or accept it, or believe it, or whatever. Reality is what I see and hear and shoot. And right now I need information about reality, not you patronizing me and lying, because I'd much rather be prepared to shoot the next fucked-up thing *before* it almost kills one of us. Are we fucking clear?"

He nodded slowly, his throat bobbing under my palm. My fingers flexed of their own volition. I was supposed to kill him. I was getting paid to kill him. Killing him before he helped me get out of this place didn't make any sense, but I ought to *want* to kill him, at least. I ought to be regretting that I couldn't just tighten my hand all the way, snap his neck, and be done with it. Job over.

The soft skin under my fingers and the perfect way my hand fit there didn't make me want to kill him. If we'd been in the back room of a club and I'd had him pinned to the wall like this, the next move would've been taking hold of his cock, or maybe sliding my hand between his legs to tease the crease of his ass. Massaging that slender throat and making him squirm.

I stepped back abruptly, releasing him and getting a few feet between us. I'd made my point, and the shit going on in my head had gotten out of control. Linden rubbed at the marks my fingers had left on the whiteness of his neck.

"It's called a kaadus, whatever that means to you," he said

with a trace of sarcasm. Okay, he'd made his point too. I really didn't have any context for this. "It's rumored to strip men's flesh from their bones and wear them until they dissolve in the kaadus's caustic innards."

Ugh. "Let's not be the ones to test that theory, yeah?" I considered the kaadus for a second. "Why don't the teeth dissolve, then?"

Linden stared at me. "Is that really your first question?"

I shrugged. "Seems relevant enough. The teeth were what was going to kill you, it looked like."

"Do I look like a dentist to you?" he snapped, his eyes narrowing with anger. "How the fuck should I know?"

It was my turn to stare at him, and despite myself, I barked out a laugh. Obscenity didn't seem right coming out of a mouth like that...although on the other hand, it seemed perfectly right, and it sent a little spark down my spine that I really, really didn't like.

"You definitely don't look like a dentist. And yeah, okay. Maybe table the teeth-dissolving question for later when we're out of here and we've got a bottle of Jim Beam." I went a couple of careful steps closer to the kaadus, now a flat, gelid layer on the floor. I nudged the side of it with the tip of my boot again. It seemed to have hardened a little as it deflated. I wasn't squeamish, but—it was probably the grossest thing I'd ever seen. "For now, let's stick with the *how many more of them are there here*, and *where is here anyway* questions. Oh, and you can tell me if you put something in that drink you made for me, too, and if it's going to kill me. And make it fucking snappy. I'm just about out of patience."

Linden drew in a deep breath, harsh and labored, and his eyes went even wider. "I didn't poison you!"

That was what he'd chosen to address first. Of course. But he sounded genuinely horrified. Christ. Looking into those eyes made it really fucking hard to imagine he'd do something like that, but I'd been hoping to hell that he had.

If he really hadn't, that meant this was…real.

My head throbbed, but I gave grudging nod. "Fine. Answer my other questions."

Linden nibbled his lip in a really goddamn distracting way, and then finally said, "We're in a different realm. This isn't the human world. And—that could be the only kaadus for miles. Or there could be dozens of them right around the corner. I don't have any way of knowing, since I've never been here before. This wasn't where I was trying to go, when I opened the portal. There are other gateways. I think the stronger magic of this one pulled us in, even though I had aimed for another. Or maybe this one had been opened more recently."

My fifth-grade teacher had done this thing when one of the students pushed him to the limit, where he took off his glasses, pinched the bridge of his nose, and shook his head slowly. I'd always thought it was over the top. As I dug my fingers into the sides of my nose and sighed, I finally got it. *A different realm.* I flashed back to another elementary-school experience, the *Dungeons and Dragons* campaign Jason had run at lunchtime. He would've loved this shit.

Okay, so not the human world, whatever the fuck that meant. That made about as much sense as a two-day hallucination, I guessed. And Linden had brought us here. Which meant…

"So you're not human." I let go of my nose, allowing the pressure to come pounding back, and looked at him. He was just standing there, his plush lips pursed into something between petulance and stubbornness. A thin line of blood had started dripping down his forearm. At least his blood wasn't green or something. "Right?"

He nodded.

"Okay. And you thought the best thing to do to escape was go through a tree without knowing exactly where you were going, ending up in a place you'd never been, that doesn't have any food or water or an obvious way out, and that's infested with flesh-stripping bone monsters. Does that about sum it up?"

There was a short pause. I thought about grabbing him by the neck again.

"I don't know your name."

"What the fuck is your obsession with names?" I took a menacing step forward, and to my surprise, he stood his ground, lifting his pointy little chin at me and glaring. It put me way too close to him, close enough that the fresh green scent I'd followed down the tunnels wafted up at me way too distractingly. He smelled like something I wanted to bury my nose in and inhale. It'd be stronger if he wasn't wearing any clothes. "Screw my name," I said, almost nose to nose with him. His eyes looked so big. *How do we get out of here?*

Linden swallowed hard, and he seemed to shrink a little, as if he couldn't keep up the front any longer. "I'm not sure we do," he whispered.

Chapter Five

Callum

I'd opted to head right instead of left at the intersection where I'd found Linden, since the tunnel the other direction went parallel to the way I'd come when I'd first set out to wander this place. I estimated I'd gone several miles, and even though we had no way to know which direction was better, I didn't feel like backtracking. So I marked up the walls with some arrows, and we set off, with Linden following my lead.

I'd asked him about the symbols, and I'd shown him the first one we came to. He'd shaken his head. "I don't read that script," he said. "But now we know why we were pulled here, at least. The one who attempted to kill me must have used this route. And that flashlight isn't for seeing in the dark. It's for showing the marks. It would have shown him the way out."

Well, that helped us not at all. I didn't reply. What was the point?

Linden seemed subdued, walking along beside but half a step behind me with his head down. His admission that we might not get out at all and his inability to read the symbols had apparently left him in a brooding funk, and I was too annoyed to bother trying to snap him out of it.

Anyway, he hadn't been exactly helpful when he'd bothered to talk so far, so there was that.

We'd gone about another two miles, I estimated, when he spoke up abruptly. "Were you going to kill me?"

Telling him that putting that question in the past tense was a little optimistic felt like too much information. "Why do you ask?"

A pause. Nothing but the faint taps of our feet on stone, and a distant dripping. I'd started to get thirsty, and the dripping irritated me twice as much because of it. The blue light of the flashlight illuminated about ten feet in front of us, and otherwise there was nothing in the world, it felt like. Fuck, but I missed Google Maps.

"You came to the shop. And then you were right there again, like you were looking for me. You're armed. Someone else who followed me and was armed was trying to kill me. I guess it feels like too much of a coincidence. But you liked the hot chocolate, so I wasn't sure."

Say what now? I glanced over my shoulder and found him chewing thoughtfully on his plump lower lip again, as if he didn't know what that did to everyone around him. The fact that he wasn't human actually made me feel better about my general mental health. He was unnaturally pretty, with the white-blond silky hair and the face and the lips and the every-graceful-thing else, and at least I knew my reaction to him wasn't me. It was him.

On the other hand, he seemed to be as mentally weird as he was physically out of the ordinary, and here I was dependent on what little information relating to our survival I could scrape out of his brain. That depressed me even more than the endless tunnels.

"The hot chocolate." I was almost afraid to make it a question. I might get an answer.

"My mother's a cook," he said. "I've inherited some of her magic. When I prepare something for someone to eat or drink, their reaction to it tells me how they feel about me. You liked the hot chocolate. I thought that meant you didn't intend to hurt me. But now I'm not so sure."

"I haven't killed you, have I?" It came out a lot sharper than I'd wanted it to. *That's guilt, Callum, you asshole. You left off the word "yet."* I told the voice in the back of my mind to shut up. I wasn't above shooting it too.

"You would have by the creek. You had the gun pointed at me. I wasn't any danger to you, so the only other reason would be that you meant to shoot me with it just because."

That stung. Just *because*? Hell no! "I'm not a psychopath or a serial killer or something," I insisted, even though by most people's definitions, I totally was. "I don't kill for fun." Almost ever. Shit. "I always have a good reason."

"Humans lie so much," Linden said softly. As if he wasn't even speaking to me, just making an observation for himself alone.

"Then I guess I'm only human. I have my reasons," I snapped, and walked a little faster. We still hadn't passed anything different. Just more stone, more damp patches, more mildewy dust.

Linden took a couple of quick steps to catch up to me and peered into my face. "Reasons. But not good ones after all?"

That hit a little too close to home, and I hated being on the defensive. I knocked it back to him. "Like you haven't been lying this whole time."

He smiled, and even out of the corner of my eye it was devastating, like it'd been in the coffee shop. Like the sun coming out of the clouds. "I haven't lied to you once."

"Like fuck you haven't," I shot back. But then he didn't answer, just hummed quietly, and I ran back through all of the things he'd said to me, looking for something I could throw in his face.

And I could think of a few things that implied something different, or skirted the boundaries of the truth, but if he'd been honest about all of the weird shit I was experiencing—and I sure as hell didn't have any better explanations—then I really couldn't think of anything.

"Okay. Maybe you haven't lied," I admitted with very poor grace. "But you've omitted a whole hell of a lot. I wasn't asking more questions because there didn't seem to be any point, but maybe if you're in a more forthcoming mood you could tell me why you don't think we're getting out of here."

"I'll answer you if you answer me. Were you going to kill me? And what's your name?"

A strange shiver went through me as he asked about my name, like the question had a lot more riding on it than something you'd give out casually to the guy who took your sandwich order. He'd been focused on the other hitman's name. And now mine. Except that he'd told me his own readily enough…and he didn't lie, but he didn't tell the whole truth, either.

"Is Linden your real name?" A faint echo of something from my childhood flitted through my head, a fairy tale or something. "Your true name?"

Linden flinched, subtly but noticeably. Gotcha.

"I'm called Linden," he said carefully.

"So no, in other words." And why did that piss me off so bad, enough that I felt pressure in my chest? Names didn't have any particular power behind them.

Unless they did, of course.

"Who calls you Linden?"

"My friends call me Linden."

"But someone else calls you something else. Something you don't want me to know?"

"There's a—fuck, you're going to think this sounds so stupid. It's really not relevant."

I didn't look like a dentist either, so why did I feel like I was pulling teeth? And I was going to need one, too, at the rate I was gritting my own.

Fuck it. "My name's Callum."

"Callum," he said meditatively, in a tone like he was rolling it around in his mouth and tasting it. The pit of my stomach clenched a little. This wasn't the time or the place, and Linden wasn't the person, damn it. I didn't even get laid that much, and when I did it was mostly women I picked up in bars where no one cared who came and went. I'd gotten used to going without during deployments, and later when I was working and keeping to myself. Why the fuck had my libido chosen this particular fucking moment to sit up and take notice?

"Yeah. Callum. Plain fucking name for a plain fucking guy. Now can we—" Ah, fuck, he'd asked two questions. What did I really have to gain by hiding the truth now? We might die of starvation here, and if we did get out, who knew what might happen? "And I was thinking about killing you. I was hired to kill you. I'm not going to kill you right now. Satisfied?"

"You answered my questions, so I suppose I have to be," he said in a soft, sad little voice. Now it was my chest clenching uncomfortably. I kept my mouth closed, forcing the apology trying to pop out to stay the fuck where it belonged. "And now you want me to answer yours. I wish I could. This place is a sort of space between worlds. I didn't mean for us to end up here. It was an accident."

The anger I'd been pushing aside rose up all of a sudden. "It wasn't an accident to take off while I was knocked out and leave me alone where we landed, though, was it? Was it even an accident that I got knocked out in the first place?"

We kept walking, the featureless floor passing under our feet stone by stone. Drip. Drip. Cold. Darkness. He didn't answer for a while.

Finally he said, "You're unaccustomed to that kind of travel, and it hit you harder than it did me. I ran because I was afraid of what you might do to me when you woke. You would have been angry. You *are* angry."

"I still saved your fucking life." I walked a little faster. I was getting hungry now in addition to thirsty, and the confirmation that Linden had brought us here by accident and had no fucking clue what he was doing, and hadn't just been holding out on me, wasn't helping.

"Yes, you did." He sighed, and then I felt a brush over my forearm. I stopped dead and looked down. He had his hand resting on me, the pressure so light it was almost nonexistent. Linden tilted his head, gazing at me with an expression I couldn't read in those big eyes. "Truce, maybe? Could we do that? I'll tell you what I can, and I won't abandon you even if the opportunity presents itself. As long as you promise you're not going to kill me. Now or later."

I looked down at him, having trouble focusing on anything but the touch of his hand. When I'd gotten this job, I'd thought the first time I touched him would be the last. I'd only need to touch him once to end him, after all, and maybe I wouldn't even have touched him at all until he was already dead. Now that felt impossible. His fingers were pale and slim. Fragile. I could crush them, crush him. I could lie and kill him later either way.

Jesse could already be dead, and I'd never know. Killing Linden wouldn't bring him back. And I knew damn well what Jesse would say. If he could see Linden, he'd tell me to make that promise and let the chips fall where they may. Jesse had originally come down on the side of finishing the job, but...he wouldn't want this. He wouldn't want me to have murdering a complete innocent on my soul.

Not that I'd ever given much thought to my soul; gun to my head, I'd have guessed I didn't have one. Jesse would think I did. Jesse always tried to see the best in the people he loved, even when we didn't deserve it.

Linden's eyes drew me in. His lips were so close.

"Yeah," I said at last. "I promise." And the relief that hit me the second I did nearly knocked me over. I hadn't wanted to kill him even before I met him. And the second I had—well, what had happened in my head the second I met him was something I didn't have the time or the inclination to get into.

But fuck, I really, really didn't want to kill him.

Linden looked into my eyes, and I couldn't tear my own gaze away. His tongue flickered out over those soft lips. He smelled like fresh green leaves in the beginning of spring, like that scent that hit you when you walked out the door after the snow melted and took a deep breath. It drowned out the stale reek of the tunnels completely for a second.

"I believe you," Linden said. "At least, I'm going to try very hard to believe you."

You can trust me. The words didn't quite make it past my lips. Yeah, I'd kill to protect him, but then again, I'd kill for a lot of reasons. That wasn't something I could really claim credit for. Technically I could've demanded his gratitude and trust in return for coming to his rescue when the kaadus nearly killed him and absorbed his bones, but did I really deserve thanks for doing something that came as naturally to me as breathing? From my perspective, I'd given him a dollar to get a cup of coffee, or held a door open for him. It wasn't a favor that deserved more than a polite nod.

Would I *die* to protect him, that was the real question.

And no. No, I wouldn't. I'd die to protect Jesse. And even that got a little fuzzy, depending on circumstances. Linden—no.

And that was the only kind of trust that mattered.

"I'm not going to kill you, no matter what," I said finally. "And if I can prevent you from being hurt or killed without dying myself, I will. We're allies while we're stuck here. No question on that. Okay?"

To my surprise, he smiled, his eyes sparkling a little even though there wasn't much light to make them glitter.

Magic. The fucker had magic, just like he'd told me. I felt crazy even thinking it, but it was so much more reasonable than any other explanation. Occam's crazy, fucked-up, hallucinatory razor.

"I accept your word," he said, his tone oddly formal, especially in contrast to his mischievous grin. "You phrase yourself with precision and you're ruthless. I think you'd fit in well where I come from."

He took his hand away from my arm at last, and I had to stop myself from grabbing it and putting it back. I only wished I wasn't wearing the damn jacket, so that I could've felt his skin on mine. I'd put my hand around his bare wrist when I dragged him out of town, but that had been my hand on him. Not his on me. It felt like a bigger difference than it was.

I shook my head, snapping myself back to my priorities.

Survival, evasion, resistance, escape. We didn't have much to evade or resist at the moment, but survival and escape were a lot more important than worrying about whether Linden wanted to touch me.

He seemed to take that head shake as aimed at him. "You would. You'd be respected in a way I never was." His smile faltered. "What do we do now?"

"I'm not the expert here," I said. "I think we've gone about six miles from where we started, not counting the little distance between the two parallel tunnels. Maybe six and a half miles total. You said this place is 'between worlds.' That means you can get in and out of the normal world through here, right? And in and out of whatever the other world is you were trying to get to." He nodded. "And obviously whatever you did to get us here isn't going to work in reverse, or you'd have done it already." Another nod. I'd started to get a little frustrated. "Do you actually have any better ideas than wandering around until we find the edge of wherever we are?"

"No. I'd hoped you did, since you seemed to know where you were going."

The top of my head nearly popped off at that. "Seemed to know where—Linden, *how the fuck* would I know where I'm going? Do you seriously think *I* can read those fucking squiggles?

And you think maybe I would've said so? I picked a direction and kept going that way, so at least we wouldn't be wandering around in circles!"

Linden lifted his chin and glared at me. He didn't seem intimidated at all, even though I'd unconsciously leaned into his space and kind of yelled right at him. Apparently he was taking my promise seriously. "Then I guess we keep doing that."

And maybe we would have, if the second he finished speaking the whole place hadn't started to shake, dust falling from the ceiling and the floor rolling and jolting under our feet, an echoing rumble rising up from everywhere at once.

Chapter Six

Callum

Linden tripped backward, his arms pinwheeling, and smacked into the wall with his mouth wide open. I flailed after him, but I couldn't catch him before he went down. He slid to the floor and I fell into a crouch, bracing myself on the rippling stone floor with my fists.

And it was rippling, buckling visibly like it'd come to life beneath us. The roar was like being right in front of a freight train, so loud it whited out my other senses. "What the fuck is this?" I shouted, though I doubted Linden could even hear me.

His mouth moved, but all I caught were snatches of sound, like he'd been badly edited.

I managed to prop myself on one hand and shine the flashlight around, for all the good it would do. All I saw was stone, shaking and waving, lit like a strobe as the beam bounced with my own motion.

Linden lurched toward me, beckoning frantically, and I launched myself in his direction, landing hard half on top of him. He wrapped his arms around my neck and yanked my head down. "Someone else is trying to get in!" he shouted right into my ear. "Someone whose magic isn't compatible with this place!"

The word "place" rang endlessly in my battered ear as the earthquake, and the noise, stopped as abruptly as it started. Then both of my ears were just ringing. I shook my head. He still had his arms locked around my neck, and our chests were pressed together. His heart thumped so hard I could feel it.

I leaned in even further, close to his ear, until his hair feathered against my cheek, and murmured, "Did they get in, or not?"

He swallowed hard. "I don't know. My magic's not strong enough to tell."

Well, that sucked, because my magic sure as fuck wasn't going to be up to the task. I opened my mouth, but whatever question I might've thought of next died on my lips.

Footsteps. That was without a doubt the sound of footsteps, and whoever or whatever was making them had shoes. Not a kaadus. I pulled back, and our eyes met, Linden's gone wide with the same realization. We had company.

I clicked off the flashlight. The last thing we needed was our company spotting us before I could get a bead on them. Leaning in again, the very minimal space between us feeling even more intimate in the pitch-blackness, I put my mouth nearly against his ear and whispered so softly I almost wasn't vocalizing.

"We're not going to move. Sound carries here and there's no cover, we're too far from a corner. Stay perfectly still."

He didn't answer me or even nod, and I smiled into the darkness. Whatever else he might be, Linden was a quick study. We held ourselves rigid, straining to hear what was coming. The heat of his body and the rise and fall of his quick breaths were distracting as hell, but I forced myself to focus. The footsteps echoed oddly. I turned my head back and forth a couple of times until I was certain they were coming from the direction we'd already been. Did that mean we were going the wrong way? Was whatever passed for an exit behind us, or did the fucked-up rules of this place have one area to land in, and one that would let you out? Hopefully I wouldn't have to kill whoever they were before we could ask them.

Nicely, if that worked. Not so nicely if it didn't. I wasn't picky at this point.

The sounds grew closer, and a murmur of voices joined the tap-tap of…two pairs of feet. All right. Two targets. I turned slowly and carefully, putting myself up against the wall between Linden and whoever was coming. My gun stayed trained straight down the tunnel.

And then my eyes picked up the faintest glow. At first I thought I was imagining it, the way you'd sometimes see lighter spots against the darkness when you closed your eyes, but it grew suddenly brighter.

That might mean they'd taken the same turn we had, at the junction where the kaadus had attacked, and now were in our stretch of tunnel.

Probably following the arrows I'd scratched on the wall, although I had no idea whether they'd arrived in the labyrinth in the same place we had. I had to chalk the arrows up to good strategy, bad tactics, and let it go. They were going to be on us in a couple of minutes whether I blamed myself or not.

I waited, my limbs loose and my mind quiet. This was more or less par for the course for me. Linden, on the other hand, was practically vibrating behind me. Not so much for him, then. I wished he could control his breathing a little better; it was loud enough that they'd be able to hear it, if they'd shut up for a second. Luckily they kept talking, their voices not quite resolving into anything I could interpret.

Linden suddenly stiffened against my back. "I know them!" he said, and God fucking damn it, loud enough for them to hear. Their voices and footsteps stopped dead.

I lunged after him, but my fingers only brushed his jeans-clad leg. Linden had already shot to his feet and trotted past me, straight into my line of fire. I jumped up and chased after him, grabbing for his arm. "Damn it, come back—"

Linden cut me off with a stream of happy-sounding words in a language I'd never heard before.

Two voices answered, surprised and pleased, and then the footsteps started again and picked up speed, the light bobbing down the tunnel toward us. Cursing under my breath, I finally got a hold of Linden and shoved him behind me. "You don't get between the gun and the target," I hissed at him. "And—will you stay put for fuck's sake—"

"They're my friends!" Linden said, trying to dodge around me. "They came to find me! No shooting." He managed to get an arm across my back and wrap his fingers around my wrist. "Callum, no shooting anyone. They can get us out of here. And they don't mean us any harm."

Right. Because our track record so far that day stood at zero for two.

Still, I lowered my weapon a little, enough that Linden might think I was giving in. I could still aim and shoot more quickly than they could react, but he wouldn't necessarily know that.

The light grew closer, and two men finally became visible. One of them was built sort of like Linden, tall and slim, only he had dark hair and was wearing something like a short dress over a pair of pants and big ridiculous boots. He looked like a refugee from a kids' book, one of the ones with talking cats and people with titles I could never pronounce. He also had some kind of stick in one hand, the light coming from a glowing bulb at the top. The other guy wore similar clothes, but he was built like a brick shithouse with long, flowing black hair, and had a sword hanging by his side that was big enough you wouldn't carry it unless you knew damn well how to use it.

The first guy kind of made me want to laugh. The second guy wasn't fucking funny at all.

He got a lot less fucking funny when Linden let go of my wrist, slipped out from behind me, and ran to fling himself into big sword dude's arms, speaking in a stream of that strange language and interrupting himself to kiss the guy on both cheeks.

Close to his mouth. A little too close to his fucking mouth.

The back of my neck prickled with irritation, and my gun came up again. That guy could snap Linden in half…and that was for sure what I was pissed about.

But he didn't. He hugged Linden back, his big hands careful as they slid up and down Linden's shoulder blades and then settled at his waist. My finger tightened a little on the trigger.

Linden finally, finally moved on to boots dude, hugging him too, though not as closely. More of a magic bro-hug. This guy's hands didn't linger quite as much, but he still managed to cop a decent feel.

And that was enough of that. "Linden," I said, low enough to be almost a growl, making sure my sights were right in the middle of the bigger guy's chest. "You going to introduce us, or what?"

"Oh," Linden said, sounding surprised. Like he'd fucking forgotten I was even there. He let go of his "friend" and spun around, his pretty lips curved in the first genuine smile I'd seen on his face all day and his blue eyes sparkling in the glow of the…glowing thing. "Callum! These are two of my closest friends. Kaspar and Oskar." He gestured first at the thin friend, and then at the too-muscled friend. "Kas, Oskar—" And then he waved his hand at me, going back to their language. I caught my name, and Oskar's frown. That told me more or less all I needed to know.

I nodded at them, and I finally lowered my gun. Appearing friendly had to be my better move at this point. If they made a wrong move of their own, though…I could aim and shoot a lot faster than Oskar could draw that sword of his.

Kaspar smiled brightly and said something that included my name. "He says he's grateful to you for saving my life this morning," Linden translated. "And for saving it again when the kaadus attacked me."

I hadn't done it for fucking Kaspar, and I couldn't bring myself to say he was welcome. "Can they get us the fuck out of here?"

Linden's smile faded, his lips curling down at the edges in a way that made me feel guiltier than him yelling at me would've done. He turned back to Kaspar, and they exchanged a few words. "Yes, they can," Linden said to me. "And we were going the right way, actually. The thin point between this place and my world isn't too much farther down the tunnel."

Well, score one for our random wandering. "Let's go, then."

I stood aside, waving them along. I wasn't putting Oskar at my back. He obviously felt the same way, and we ended up in a back-and-forth game of chicken.

"Tell Oskar to lead the way," I said, without taking my eyes off the man. "I'll take rear guard."

It was the safest way to go, and also the most practical. And it put Linden and Kaspar between my gun and Oskar's back, which might make him likelier to go along with it, though it made me twitchy as fuck. Oskar grunted agreement after Linden translated, gave me the stink-eye, and took point.

Linden and Kaspar actually linked arms, strolling along in the middle like we were in the park or something. They chattered away, laughing now and then. Their language sounded vaguely Scandinavian, but it wasn't one I could place. *Not a human language*, the back of my mind supplied. *Because they're not fucking human.*

At least they weren't made out of murderous Jell-O. I stalked along behind them, glowering at nothing in particular—especially not the way Linden kept tipping his head until it almost rested on Kaspar's shoulder.

Oskar stopped abruptly, and the rest of us barely avoided a pile-up behind him. I almost ran into Linden's back, and I felt the warmth of him. His hair brushed my nose. I got another hit of his body's fresh scent. Fuck, it was like a drug. I forced myself to take a step back.

Tweedledee and Tweedledum bent their heads together, muttering over a flagstone that looked exactly the fucking same as every other flagstone.

In the light of the glowing staff thing, anyway.

I pulled out the flashlight and shone it onto the stone they were looking at. Sure enough, it lit up with a twisty, glowing symbol like the others I'd seen.

All of a sudden three pairs of eyes were fixed on me, two in obvious suspicion.

"What?" I switched the apparently magic flashlight off, feeling both smug and kind of silly. I'd picked up a couple of fantasy novels while I was deployed, old tattered paperbacks kicking around the FOB, remnants of a long-ago care package from someone's mom, probably. The heroes of those always had some magical thingamajig, a sword or a crown or a diamond or some fancy shit like that.

Not a plastic flashlight. Then again, I wasn't any damn hero.

Linden said a few words to his friends in their language, and they both nodded, looking less confused, although Oskar still had his glare turned up to eleven. Not that I expected that to change anytime soon, no matter what Linden told him.

Kaspar shrugged, gave me a funny look, and said something in reply, gesturing at the floor. Linden sighed. "I explained that you got it from the one from our realm. And Kaspar would like you to turn it on again," he said. "Being able to see the sigil clearly will help them get us out of here."

Well, I was all for that. I clicked the button and aimed the flashlight back at the flagstone. The three of them bent over it and muttered, Kaspar tracing the sigil with his fingers.

The stone glowed more brightly, the floor started to shake, and Kaspar wrapped his free hand around Linden's wrist while Oskar grabbed the arm holding the staff. Linden snagged me by the arm in turn, and the whole world jolted and melted, like wax running down a shaken candle. With a tremendous, ear-shattering pop, the tunnel disappeared. I blinked to clear my vision and took a deep breath. Fresh grass, something flowery and sweet in the air, and above us, a huge dark sky dotted with brilliant stars.

The moon was twice as large as it should've been, and also faintly purple.

Welcome to fairyland, Callum. Fuck. All I could do was brace myself for the next surprise.

Chapter Seven

Linden

My first breath of home felt like the first breath I'd taken in weeks, full stop. No taint of lead and petroleum and plastic and tar...only rain-freshened grass and the sweep of wind down from the moonlit, snow-painted mountains. Beside me, Callum could only have been more alert, wary, and ready to kill the next comer if he'd been a wolf growling and raising its hackles. He held his appropriated flashlight like a weapon, although he held his actual weapon down by his side, in a way that didn't fool me in the least.

I'd briefly interacted with the odd realm humans called the internet while hiding in their world, and I'd run across a joke about a serial killer with a pencil and a cheerleader with something called a bazooka, and their relative ability to inspire fear. I'd had to search for nearly every word in order to figure out roughly what it meant, and I still hadn't been sure I'd understood it.

Now I did. I could have wielded the most fearsomely razor-sharp enchanted sword in any of the realms, and I wouldn't be half the threat Callum was holding a flashlight. His gun was the least of it.

"We're not safe here," Oskar said briskly, snapping me out of my thoughts. "We need cover for what's left of the night, and we need to talk, Linden."

Ah, *we need to talk*. No matter the realm or the language, no one enjoyed hearing that.

I started to reach out with a trickle of magic, trying to get a feel for where precisely we were, and Kaspar whacked me in the arm. "Don't be a fool!"

Suddenly Callum was somehow between me and Kaspar, even though there'd only been a foot of space there. His eerily calm, silent looming somehow said more than words could have.

I craned my neck and saw Kaspar very wisely taking a step back, eyes wide.

"He's my friend," I told Callum again. I appreciated the man's willingness to keep our bargain and protect me, but—wait a moment, hadn't our deal only lasted until we escaped from the labyrinth between worlds? Or had I misunderstood? I wasn't going to be the one to remind him he was no longer required to be on my side, but at the same time...at the same time, I was home, and these were my friends, my oldest friends, whom I'd played with as a boy and confided in as a youth. Having them at odds with Callum would be, for lack of a better word, exhausting. And I was already so exhausted I'd started to sway on my feet. "Don't you have friends? Who hit you in the arm when you're doing something stupid?"

Callum's back looked so broad and sturdy. I could lean on it. Maybe he'd let me climb on and sleep with my head on his shoulder while he carried me wherever Oskar meant to lead us. And it was right there, close enough that I could feel the warmth of him in contrast to the chilly bite of the evening. The pull I felt to him was more confusing than pleasant, knowing as I did how close he'd come to ending my life. But I couldn't forget the look on his face as he drank the magical hot chocolate I'd forced on him. Surprise, and delight, and a softness that had been markedly absent before and since. A voice in the back of my head kept whispering that perhaps he'd have that same look on his face if he tasted *me*. I shivered, and it wasn't the cold.

Callum sidestepped a little so that he could glance at me while still keeping a wary eye on Kaspar. "You weren't doing anything."

"I was trying to use magic, which would be the fastest way for anyone hunting me to find and track me. He felt it. You didn't. He was right to stop me, and if you want to stay alive here, you ought to pay attention to the people who know more about this realm than you do." I was too tired to be tactful.

He frowned at me, but his posture eased a trifle. "We're in your realm, now?" I nodded. "Fine. I'll—take a step back. A small step," he said sharply, as I started to smile in relief. "I don't trust them. For that matter, I don't trust you."

"I'd be surprised if you did," I said with a sigh. "Just please don't kill them. We need them. And I'm—attached to them. They're my oldest friends." He didn't look all that pleased. I tried again. "They're like brothers to me."

And, oddly, that wiped the frown off Callum's face. He barked out a laugh. "At least I'm managing expectations. Fine. What's next?"

Oskar and Kaspar had been muttering to one another, with Kaspar digging around in the satchel slung over his shoulder, while I got Callum in line. I turned to them. "Where are we going?"

"Do you remember my grandfather's hunting lodge?" Oskar asked me. And then it made sense. I hadn't recognized the place right away because we generally approached the lodge from the other side, and we rarely came down into this valley, only looking at it from above and from the opposite direction. But with a quick reorientation of my perspective, I recognized my surroundings at last.

"We'll have to cross that river, won't we?" I couldn't help my tone of dismay, and Kaspar laughed at me, the bastard.

But he also handed me a chunk of bread and a piece of cheese, and gave me a drink from the water canteen he'd taken out of his bag. I fell on it like a starving beast. He handed the same to Callum, who eyed it for a moment, shrugged, and then dug in.

In a spray of crumbs, I explained the route to Callum: over the river and up the hill into the forest. There were nods all around, and we set off.

I'd expected to walk in the same order we'd been in while in the labyrinth, but as I tried to fall into step with Kaspar, he shook his head and grimaced at me. "Your guard dog's not going to be happy unless he has you closer than that," he said. My guard dog? My mouth fell open, but Kaspar went on. "And I don't fancy having him staring a hole in the back of my neck while I talk to you. It feels like being one step ahead of Death."

He took point with Oskar, letting his light lead the way, and I set out with Callum at my side. I glanced at him as we walked. He did seem more relaxed, though it couldn't possibly be because he was walking with me rather than watching me walk with Kaspar, could it? When I stumbled over an uneven clump of grass, his hand shot out and wrapped around my arm.

And then he left it there, his fingers strong and firm. When he'd pulled me out of the town and into the woods in the human realm, his grip had felt like a threat. It had *been* a threat. This was different, and I wanted to lean into him the way I would've leaned into Kaspar, taking comfort from physical closeness and the sense of security provided by not being alone.

I couldn't shake the feeling that I was safe with Callum, whether or not it was true.

Oh, the hell with it. I shifted a little closer, so that our bodies were almost brushing as we walked. Callum's stride stayed as determined as ever. He didn't seem to be flagging at all, even though we'd both gone the ancestors only knew how long without food, water, or sleep, and were now getting by on the strength of a few bites of bread. Time didn't have much meaning in the labyrinth, but my aching stomach and feet knew it had been longer than they preferred.

"Aren't you tired?" I asked him quietly. "Or hungry for something better than bread and water?"

I felt his shrug as his arm shifted. "Yes. But it's irrelevant until I can do something about it."

My stomach chose that moment to make its feelings known, loudly. Maybe Callum was satisfied, but my belly was *not*. "I wish I could ignore it too."

"I've had a lot of practice." His tone didn't invite further questions.

All right, we didn't need to talk. But that didn't prevent me from wanting more than trudging along side by side in silence. It would be a good self-protective measure to keep him invested in my safety and well-being. I'd tell myself that over and over if I needed to, to drown out the insistent little voice saying what I wished I could deny: that I wanted to be closer, the danger be damned. I'd seen how intent Callum could be, how focused. I wanted that focus on me, even if there was danger in it.

Perhaps especially if there was danger in it. The nice, quiet young men I'd known at home had never excited me—a flaw in my fundamental make-up, I'd always assumed. Callum's hand around my throat had made me ache in ways I couldn't bear to acknowledge. The contrast of it…he could hurt me, or he could choose not to. At home, where options were limited, would-be lovers approached me because there weren't many others. I wanted to be someone's choice. I wanted the thrill of the full attention of a man who could've dismissed me, who could've killed me.

Clearly I had something broken in me, but right then I couldn't care about it. All I wanted was to sleep, secure in the knowledge that Callum would be watching over me. He had to be exhausted too, no matter how well he hid it. Perhaps that made me selfish on top of broken.

We'd crested a small rise and were temporarily going

downhill now, with another small valley spread out beneath us. The moon and stars here shone so much brighter than in the human realm, even after accounting for the light pollution of human cities. Bigger, and somehow sparklier, glinting like diamonds in the dark velvet of the night sky. Even the sky itself had more texture, more presence. At the bottom of the hill a shallow river wound its way between grassy banks, the wet rocks along the edges and sticking up in the middle throwing out faint blue and pink gleams in the moonlight and smaller glimmers from the beams of the stars.

Ahead of us, Oskar and Kaspar stepped apart slightly to avoid a little hillock. I saw it, but I pretended I didn't, letting my foot catch on it and tripping with a quiet cry of 'surprise.'

Callum let go of my arm and caught me around the waist, cinching me against his side before I could do more than sway toward the ground. "Careful," he said, his voice unusually rough. "If you break a leg, I don't think there are any hospitals around here."

I smiled, my head tipped down so he couldn't see my face. There. Concern. Care, even. This man wouldn't kill me, I was sure of it.

He could, but he wouldn't.

And his arm around me felt so good. I leaned into it, leaned into him. His body had a solidity that mine lacked—not that I felt I lacked anything, really. My body was just right as it was. And his fit just right against mine.

We stayed that way until we reached the river, where we had to separate to pick our way across the ford Oskar pointed out, a path across where the gravel bed rose high enough to make the water no more than knee-deep. But he was there again as I sloshed up the opposite bank, my very human sneakers waterlogged and squishing with every step. Without comment, he slipped his arm around me again as if it was the most natural thing in the world.

Trees closed in around us as we made our way up the hill.

We paused after a few hundred yards while Oskar looked around, finding the almost-hidden path through the woods. He grunted in satisfaction and led us a little to the left. Finally, as my eyes were blinking closed more often than blinking open again and I no longer needed to pretend to stumble, we stepped out into the small clearing that held the lodge, which was little more than a mossy-roofed, dilapidated cottage.

My eyes tried to slide shut again, and I forced them open for a second. My eyelids drooped. Callum was carrying me more than walking with me, and my head kept bouncing onto his shoulder as I tried to lift it up again. Ancestors, but my legs were made of granite. Aching, burning granite. A headache throbbed in my temples.

"Linden, are you all right?" Kaspar. He sounded annoyingly awake. Of course, he'd probably had a full night's sleep and a meal before his visit to the labyrinth, the bastard. "Is he hurting you?"

"I'm fine," I mumbled into Callum's shoulder. "Just let him put me to bed. Please tell me there is a bed, and we're not sleeping on bedrolls." I hadn't been to the lodge in years, and I had no idea what improvements Oskar had made in the meantime.

"For a certain value of bed," Kaspar grumbled, and Oskar cut in with, "I didn't see you contributing anywhere to sleep for the night, Kas."

We shuffled inside, Callum maneuvered me through the damp, chilly front room that seemed to hold more spiders than furniture, food, or cheer—hoping for improvements since the last time I'd been here had clearly been too optimistic—and then I was lying down on something dusty but softer than a flagstone or bare earth.

Sleep sucked me into its vortex almost instantly, but I had time to smile over Kaspar and Oskar's familiar grousing, and then to have that smile fade away as I realized I was going to sleep, leaving them with Callum. Who didn't speak their language, or the other way around.

Well, fuck.
I fell asleep anyway.

Chapter Eight

Callum

Linden had told me we were going to a hunting lodge, which didn't mean a lot to me. I wasn't the sort of guy who had friends with vacation houses. Safe houses, yeah, but you went there when someone hunted you, not the other way around. The reality came closer to a deer blind with a door than to a holiday cabin. Two small rooms, one with a fireplace and a wooden table and a single rough chair, and the other with an even rougher low wooden frame holding a lumpy mattress and a couple of wool blankets.

I laid Linden down on the pathetic excuse for a bed reluctantly, unwilling to let him out of my grasp. For all I knew he'd vanish in a puff of vaporized tree, or get eaten, the second I let go.

He didn't. He smiled, his face relaxing into the sleepy sweetness of someone who didn't have a care in the world, and passed the fuck out almost instantly.

Well, nice for him. Not that he was wrong. I wasn't going to let anything happen to him.

I turned and met two identical disapproving glares. Tweedledee and Tweedledum clearly weren't too happy with me.

Kaspar gestured with his glowing staff and said a few words, and Oskar waved his hands at me, clearly trying to herd me back into the other room. Fine. We could all leave Linden to sleep, but I wasn't leaving either of them alone with him.

I made a gesture of my own, though not the one I really wanted to. *You first*. Frowning, they edged out of the room backward, watching me to make sure I followed them. They obviously felt the same way.

Even with my stamina, the day had started to take its inevitable toll. I crouched down by the doorway into Linden's bedroom, taking a load off by letting my back rest against the wall. I couldn't risk sitting down, let alone lying down, with these two wide awake and looking at me like they were sizing me up for Oskar's sword.

They turned away and spoke amongst themselves for a couple of minutes, arguing in low voices. Finally Kaspar set the leather bag he'd had slung on his back onto the table and pulled out a small cloth bag, waving his hand over it and muttering a few words. The bag glowed pinkish-white, vibrated, and—started to grow. My hand tightened on the gun in my front pocket. I'd had enough of magical bags for one fucking day, thank you.

But it didn't do anything threatening, just got bigger until it was the size of the original leather bag it'd come out of.

Kaspar reached in and pulled out more bread and cheese, some apples, a small cloth-wrapped package, and a bottle that gleamed an odd greenish-yellow. Wine, maybe? Either way, and even though I didn't trust these two not to poison, drug, or magic-whammy me, my stomach growled. The snack they'd handed out when we got out of the labyrinth had helped, but I felt like I could eat a horse, let alone another round of bread.

Oskar laughed, shaking his head, and spoke to me directly for the first time. I couldn't understand him, but it almost sounded friendly.

Almost.

But instead of handing more food around, Kaspar unfolded the cloth package to reveal what looked like little cakes or cookies.

And then the argument started up again. From their tones, Kaspar was trying to talk Oskar into something he thought was a bad idea. At last Kaspar threw his hands up and said something that sounded, in any language, like *I'm doing it anyway*, and pointed one finger at one of the cakes. It too glowed faintly pink.

Kaspar picked up the cake and brought it over to me, waving it at me as if to say, *Here, take this fucked-up glowing fairy food and eat it, no worries, what could possibly go wrong?* I stared at him in disbelief. Did I have a sign taped to my forehead saying I was a fucking moron or something?

He held it out again, sounding frustrated. With the other hand, he pointed at his own mouth and then at his ear. Then pointed at me, and then at his ear again, raising his eyebrows.

Okay. I'd landed somewhere magic was the norm. Linden somehow knew how to speak English despite coming from this place, and he hadn't been in California long enough to be as fluent as he was, especially without even a trace of an accent.

How had that happened? Magic, almost certainly. If I was reading Kaspar right, he was trying to indicate speaking and hearing. He wanted me to eat the cake. With a little luck, it'd make me able to understand their language, and maybe speak it too. Without it, I'd spend the rest of my bitter, self-hating life as a frog in that river down the hill. I seemed to remember someone in a fairy tale being turned into a frog, and it seemed as likely as anything else.

Kaspar sighed, shook his head, and turned to Oskar. They argued some more. Finally, grousing all the while, Oskar started to unbuckle his belt.

Okay, and that was taking an unexpected fucking turn. I tensed and made sure my thumb rested on the safety of the Beretta.

Oskar took off his belt, carefully held his sword across his two outstretched hands, and nodded to me before setting the sword on the table. He backed away and spread his hands. He looked fucking miserable about it, too, and kept shooting death-glares at Kaspar.

Kaspar nodded, said something in an exasperated tone, and then tried to hand the cake to me again.

This time I took it. They were trying. They clearly did care about Linden, and he trusted them. And if this—oatmeal cookie?—would somehow let me communicate with them, that was all to the good. I was stuck with them.

It might still be poisoned. I wouldn't be shocked. But I didn't have a lot of options.

Fuck it.

I stuck the damn thing in my mouth and chewed. It had the texture and almost exactly the same flavor as every other MRE bar I'd ever choked down. If my mouth hadn't been stuffed with chewy sawdust, I might've laughed, because apparently no matter what realm you were in, soldiers always had shitty rations. It was oddly reassuring.

Nothing happened after I forced the thing down. No stomach cramps, my throat didn't close up, and I didn't keel over.

But it also didn't feel like magic.

And then Kaspar said, "You ought to be able to understand me now. Can you?"

I could tell he wasn't speaking English, but I could under-stand him. Like I'd become fluent in whatever language he was speaking without ever going through the intervening steps of fig-uring out a few words, getting a hang of the grammar, and build-ing from there. I spoke mostly fluent Dari, and I could get by in Russian and Spanish, so learning another language wasn't new to me.

This was, though. Magic was wild.

"Yeah, I can," I said, and as I did, I knew I wasn't speaking English, either. That felt even more bizarre.

Kaspar grinned at me, and then turned to Oskar. "I told you I could do it!"

The smile I hadn't realized I was wearing fell away. "You didn't know that would work? What the fuck? What would've happened if you were wrong?"

"Nothing. Probably," Kaspar said. "It's a basic spell, infusing a language into a spell-cake. I made it for you rather than making cakes for us, since you need to know the language to infuse it."

"A spell-cake." I was officially not fucking amused. "A cake that...holds spells. That's what it's for?" Kaspar nodded. "You could've put any damn spell on it, then."

Maybe I needed the idiot sign on my forehead after all. Jesus fucking Christ. I didn't scare easily, but a chill went down my spine. I wasn't in Kansas anymore. And I wasn't the one in control of this situation, no matter how hard I tried to pretend. I needed to readjust my thought patterns, stat. I'd been so focused on Oskar's visible, very blatant weapon that I'd overlooked Kaspar's fucking *magic*, dismissing it as—what? A figment of my imagination? Something that I'd never believed in, so it couldn't be real?

I damn well knew better than that.

"Is he all right?" Oskar, whose rumbly voice didn't hold even a thread of genuine concern. He sounded more like he wanted to evaluate my potential threat level if I lost my shit.

And that snapped me out of it. That, I could understand. I didn't trust Oskar any more than he trusted me, but he was taking my measure the same way I was doing with him. He thought like a soldier. And I could work with that. Use it. I looked up at him, pushed myself off the wall, and stood.

"You don't need to waste your time worrying about me," I said. "It sounds like Linden's the one you ought to be focusing on."

Kaspar and Oskar exchanged a look, and I held my breath. Linden hadn't told me what was going on. If he'd been any cagier, he could've been in a zoo. But these two clearly knew, and if they thought I did too...well, then I could get Oskar, at least, focused on the goal, and get him talking. If I couldn't get information from

Linden, then maybe I could squeeze it out of his friends.

"All we can do right now is hide him," Kaspar said at last. "I can track his magic more accurately than anyone else can, since I know it so well. I felt it when he moved between realms, and we followed the trace into the labyrinth. But others might be able to trace him too, though not as quickly. And there are only two of us to protect him. His enemies are far more numerous."

"Three of us," I corrected him, only realizing how much I meant it as the words fell out of my mouth. Fuck. Oskar frowned and Kaspar looked thoughtful. "Linden didn't have time to give me a lot of detail," I lied. "What are we up against?"

And why, and…if I'd had the option of asking all the questions I really wanted answered, we'd have been there all week. But I couldn't think of a better option to get them talking, and hopefully I'd be able to fill in some of the blanks.

Although given the total strangeness of the whole situation, I'd need to be careful what I assumed. Fuck, what a headache in the making. This was worse than trying to pry useful intel out of an officer.

Kaspar sighed. "Lord Evalt's strength hasn't grown since Linden left to hide in your realm, and in fact he's suffered some setbacks. But that only means he's more obsessed with Linden than he was before. He wants him dead, as quickly as possible. We thought Linden would be safer there than here, due to the Courts' edicts. But Linden said you saved his life when an assassin made an attempt on him there?"

"Yeah. And I'm not sure that guy was totally human, either." I'd thought he was at the time, but I could go either way on that. And if these two weren't already thinking 'hired human killer,' I wanted to keep it that way. "Did Lord Evalt send him? If he did, then he already knew where Linden was."

Which was, of course, one of the few pieces of the puzzle I'd already had. Lord Evalt, whoever he was, must've sent the assholes who hired Jesse and me. Obviously he'd found Linden.

"Someone told Lord Evalt that Linden had gone to the human realm," Oskar put in, with a suspicious glare at me. "Someone is spying on him."

I chose to answer the subtext. "Do I look like someone Lord Evalt would be in bed with?"

They both stared at me. "As far as I know, Lord Evalt takes only female lovers," Kaspar said dubiously.

Right. I might be fluent in their language, but that didn't mean I had any grasp on their idioms. I'd translated one of my own directly, without stopping to think about it. "Figure of speech. I'm not magical and I can't track anyone with magic. I don't think I'm Lord Evalt's type, in bed or out of it."

"Very few in the human realm are magical," Oskar rumbled. "Even a sorcerer like Lord Evalt must use mundane tools when working there."

If I got back to my own world alive and ever saw Jesse again, I had to remember to tell him some frowning fucker with a giant sword had called me a 'mundane tool.' I'd never hear the end of it, but it'd be worth it to see him grin.

"Yeah, well, I'm not working for anyone except myself." Anymore. "I want to get back to my own world. I can tell you don't trust me. Fine. I wouldn't trust me either. If you want to get rid of me, send me home. If you can't send me home, then you might as well try to work with me."

And why was I now mentally crossing my fingers that they *couldn't* send me home? Jesus fucking Christ. Jesse might be dead or on the run, one step ahead of being killed. He should've been my priority.

On the other hand, if the source of our problems lay here in this realm, then dealing with it here might be the only way to end it. If this Evalt character was pulling strings in my world, I had to cut them.

"We can't send you home right away," Kaspar said. He sat down in the room's one chair with a sigh, and Oskar and I had a moment of understanding as we both eyed him with annoyance. "The only way I know how to use without risking an accident is through the labyrinth, but that's too easy to track. Lord Evalt will be watching it now that it's been used twice in such quick succession. And Linden's magic isn't really strong enough to travel between realms. You're both lucky you weren't stranded somewhere worse."

Oskar hadn't gone for his sword again, and fuck, but I was getting tired by now. I propped myself up against the wall and risked crossing my arms, taking my hand off my gun in the process. It didn't surprise me that they couldn't send me home; I'd guessed as much. And I also guessed that Oskar, at least, would've been all for booting me out of his realm as fast as he could, if he could.

"Linden didn't get a chance to tell me exactly why Evalt's after him," I said as casually as I could manage. "If I'm not going anywhere, then you might as well fill me in while Linden's sleeping."

Kaspar opened his mouth—yes, good, someone was *finally* going to tell me what the fuck was going on—and then Oskar cut him off. "We all need to sleep while we can," he said. Which, yes. But fuck. "Eat, sleep, regroup in the morning. We'll have a long march ahead of us. Plenty of time for everyone to say his piece." Oskar leveled me with an ominous stare as he said the last few words. Clearly, he expected me to talk too. He was going to be disappointed, but I didn't bother telling him that.

Kaspar nodded and shared out the food, leaving enough for Linden when he woke. They offered me whatever was in the bottle, but I turned it down in favor of water. The last thing I needed was more fairy shit fucking me up.

The inside of the hunting lodge held almost the same chill as the outside, and all we had were bare floorboards. I'd slept rougher than that by far, though, and settled down next to the wall outside the room where Linden slept. Kaspar and Oskar took their own sections of floor, with Oskar arranging himself right across the front door. I approved. Kaspar grumbled a little, but at last he went still, and silence settled over the lodge, broken only by everyone's breathing and the faint and distant hoot of an owl.

Part of me wanted to stay on watch. I didn't trust these fuckers, I didn't know what other dangers there could be—but I'd be useless if I didn't get some rest. I closed my eyes and forced myself under.

Plenty of time to be suspicious in the morning.

Chapter Nine

Linden

My stomach woke me up by trying to do a somersault, turn inside out, and strangle me. Ancestors, but I'd have given every bit of magic I possessed for the sort of breakfast my mother always made: stewed fruit and fluffy sweet breads, tea and juice and buttered oatcakes. Another growl from my belly forced me up. Unfortunately, my magical abilities wouldn't stretch to conjuring a feast, and I'd have been suicidal to try to use magic anyway. In his own realm, Lord Evalt's sorcery would be far harder to evade.

That thought left me fighting a headache as well as a bellyache. The night before, I'd been too tired to think, too tired even to worry. Exhaustion had pushed away longing for my mother's embrace, and desperate homesickness, and terror for my family and my friends. And for myself.

But now, a little bit of light filtered in through the high, narrow window in the lodge's small bedchamber, enough to show me dawn had come. It was a new day. My troubles couldn't be put off any longer.

Near-silence still reigned, though. Even the birds hadn't fully woken yet. Soft snores filtered in from the next room, and I smiled despite everything. Kaspar always snored, and I'd have recognized that long snorting build with the small hitch at the end anywhere, after years of bunking together on excursions like this.

Only those had been for pleasure, not because I was running away from a powerful magician hell-bent on killing me to satisfy his interpretation of a prophecy.

Breakfast. Surely everything would seem less miserable after…I rubbed my hands over my chilled face. Slightly stale bread and a piece of cheese, probably. Well. Unlikely that I'd be significantly less miserable, then. But I'd prefer it to starving to death before Lord Evalt could murder me.

Freezing cold slapped my skin once I crawled out from under the blankets, not that I'd been cozy with them on. Why hadn't Oskar kept this place up at all? It'd been a little unwelcoming even when we'd visited before—but then again, we'd been better supplied.

A little twinge of guilt for my mental complaints hit me as I peeked out into the main room. All three of my companions lay stretched out on the bare, dusty floor, and not one of them had a blanket at all, let alone two. I jumped as Callum woke and rolled into a crouch all within half a second. Was the man half cat?

I knocked into the doorframe, waking Kaspar and Oskar, who both stirred and sat up. "Good morning, Callum," I said in English, a little sheepishly. I knew a blush had spread over my cheeks; at least my face wasn't cold anymore. It was embarrassing enough to stumble into a wall, but looking at Callum only made it infinitely worse. He'd been unshaven the day before, and now he had the sort of several-day stubble that would scratch perfectly against my throat, or my chest, or my inner thighs.

By the time I forced those thoughts away, my face could've cooked an egg, if we'd had one available.

"You're clumsy this morning," Oskar said, with perfect, humiliating timing.

"Well, I woke up cold and hungry," I retorted in my own language. "You could at least have let Callum share the bed with me.

He's big enough to keep me warm." Kaspar opened his mouth and started to protest, a strange expression on his face, but I barreled right over him. "And I thought we were past you two trying to protect me by keeping attractive men out of my bed! I'm grown up, aren't I?"

A strange silence fell. All three of them stared at me. Callum had a look in his eyes I couldn't interpret at all. As if he'd...as if he'd understood me.

"I made Callum a spell cake last night," Kaspar finally said. "So that he could speak to us."

Another silence. "Oh," I said faintly. The top of my head buzzed, and my cheeks could've fried every egg in the realm. "I was—I was joking," I stammered, staring down at my feet. I couldn't look up and meet Callum's eyes, even though I could feel the weight of his gaze.

"I need to take a piss," Callum said into the charged silence, rose, and headed for the door. Oskar had to scramble out of his way. Callum practically stepped on him to get the door open, shoved through it, and shut it hard behind him.

I didn't know what reaction I'd have liked to announcing to the room that I'd wanted Callum to sleep with me, but I *did* know that wasn't it.

"What an asshole," Oskar said. "And you're better off without the complication. I still think there's a better than even chance he's Evalt's spy. And," he went on mercilessly, "I don't believe you told us everything yesterday. Your story about meeting Callum in the first place had a few holes."

I swallowed hard. My story had been—not a fabrication, because the magic in my blood prevented that. But I'd left out more than I'd told. I'd emphasized Callum saving me from the other assassin, and glossed over why he'd been there in the first place as much as I could. And yesterday, I'd gotten away with it, since we'd only had a few minutes to talk between the efforts of getting out of the labyrinth and hiking to the lodge.

ELIOT GRAYSON

But now I had Oskar's full attention. And he could be relentless. It made him a fearsome opponent in a fight, and a troublesome opponent in an argument.

"He's not spying for Lord Evalt," I said. That I did believe. He'd been sent to kill me, not inform on me. Yes, he'd tried to shake as much information out of me as he could, but it was the kind he wouldn't have needed if he was Evalt's spy. "He promised he wouldn't hurt me." That came out sounding more plaintive than confident.

"And why would he need to do that?" Oskar said after an ominous pause. He stalked toward me, frowning. I knew him too well to be afraid of him, but ancestors, I was really starting to get a headache. "If he didn't mean you any harm in the first place, as you strongly implied."

"Besides, humans lie," Kaspar said, finally getting to his feet himself. "We talked a bit last night. I don't know if I believed a single word out of his mouth."

"Why did he have to promise not to hurt you?" Oskar demanded again. "I agree with Kaspar, but getting more information out of that bastard's not worth the effort. *You* owe us the truth, Linden."

My temples throbbed, and my stomach let out a pitiful grumbling howl. "Please can we not," I whispered. "Right now, he's on our side. My side. He has a friend at home who may be in danger because he's helping me. He wants to end this so he can go home and get his own affairs in order. Please don't ask me any more questions."

Oskar opened his mouth, probably to ask many, many more questions—and then Callum opened the door, and Oskar spun on his heel to glare at him instead of me. Callum's gaze flicked to me for a moment and then settled on Oskar. I felt like withering into the floor, covering my face with my arms, and pretending I couldn't see or hear any of them. My few hours of sleep hadn't been anything like enough, and all I wanted was to sleep until all of this went away.

Which wasn't like me at all. On the day of my birth, precisely at midsummer, my mother had labored all throughout an unseasonably rainy morning. She pushed me into the world at the exact moment of midday, and as I let out my first cry, the clouds broke and sun poured through, a dazzling shaft of light that set all the raindrop-laden leaves and flowers glittering like jewels. I'd stopped crying, blinked in the sunlight, and smiled.

That was how I'd earned my real name, the one my mother called me only when we were alone: Laikesev. If I'd translated it into English, it would've roughly come out to Sunlight One.

I'd lived up to it. I was almost always cheerful, not only because everyone expected it of me but because I always found something to enjoy, no matter the weather or the company or the place. It was my blessing, although the coincidence of Lord Evalt's seer having a vision of a man bringing light who would be Lord Evalt's doom had made it my curse, as well. But mostly it was a blessing. Happiness, for me, had never been dependent on circumstance. It came from within me.

So what did a man do when he couldn't be happy? I didn't have a frame of reference. This thick, weary, despairing weight on my chest and in my heavy head felt like more than I could carry. I'd been afraid when I ran from home, afraid and homesick in that little California town, and terrified in the labyrinth. But none of it had felt quite real. It was like watching an illusion of someone else's life, with all my emotions kept behind glass.

Now I'd come home. The air carried all the familiar scents of my realm's trees and grasses and shy wildflowers, the sounds of birds I could identify, the indefinable essence of my own world. I'd grown up with Kaspar and Oskar. They were as real to me as my mother or my bedroom in Lady Lisandra's manor, as real as the ivy tendrils creeping through the casement of that bedroom's single, low-set window.

If Lord Evalt found me with them, we would all die. Kaspar's blood spilling at my feet would be real. Oskar's final battle-cry as he swung his sword at our enemies before they overwhelmed him and brought him down would be real. My mother's grief...at least I hopefully wouldn't be there to see it. And I'd be far enough away from her that she wouldn't die with me.

That reminder of what was at stake washed away the sticky mire of misery I'd allowed myself to sink into.

I had to be stronger than this. My friends had risked their lives to come and find me, and they deserved better than to plan and fight and struggle for someone too pathetic to do more than mope. And Callum...I finally got up the courage to look at Callum. He and Oskar hadn't stopped eyeing one another like two testy cockerels in a farmyard.

My chest gave a painful squeeze. Callum had been hired to kill me. I'd been truly terrified of him, as he dragged me out of town with his gun pointed at me, no matter what his reaction to my magic in the hot chocolate had been. And I'd run from him in the labyrinth when I'd had the chance, when his non-magical being had been knocked unconscious by the journey. My magic hadn't been strong enough to make the journey smoother, the way Kaspar could.

But he'd promised not to hurt me. And he'd even told me he'd defend me, protect me. He hadn't asked to go home to his own realm.

On the other hand...he wanted answers. Information. He hadn't come here out of loyalty to me, and building some fantasy in my head that he'd want to stay and help me was neither rational nor fair. He didn't owe me anything.

"Oskar," I said, and my voice came out stronger than I expected. "He's not going to explode if you stop staring at him for ten seconds."

"You don't know that," Oskar growled.

"Yes, I do!" I protested, the headache surging. Ancestors, I was so hungry and so chilly and so dirty, and I hated being at odds with my best friends. I hated everything about this. "He's not going to hurt any of us—"

"Unless he's lying to you!" Oskar shouted. "Unless he's Evalt's agent. Your story doesn't add up!" He spun back to Callum, taking a menacing step forward. "And last night, trying to question Kaspar and me—you weren't as subtle as you thought you were. I want to know what the bloody buggering fuck you're doing here, and what neither of you will tell me!"

Oskar had gotten so close to Callum they were almost breathing each other's air, and Kaspar moved forward, trying to pull Oskar away, saying something meant to defuse the situation.

It wasn't going to work. I could feel it. They were going to finally come to blows, and I couldn't do anything about it—

"I used to be a soldier," Callum said abruptly. His face stayed a blank, neutral mask, and I couldn't read anything of what might be going on behind his steady dark gaze. Oskar froze, staring at him. Callum took a deep breath. "With allegiances. Loyalties. To my country, to my unit, to my officers, when they weren't useless dipshits straight out of school." Oskar shook his head and snorted a laugh, and then looked pissed to have been caught agreeing with Callum about something. "Not anymore," Callum went on with grim intensity. "I'm loyal to myself and to one man I work with and trust. You can't trust me to work against my own interests. That's not fucking happening anymore in this lifetime. You want the truth?"

Oh no, oh no, and I opened my mouth to intervene after all—but too late. "Someone hired me to kill Linden. Someone who probably would've killed me too, and my associate. I didn't want to take the job, but it didn't look like I had much choice. Well, now whoever it is will kill me no matter what, because I fucked up the job and helped Linden get away from my competition. My friend's in the wind, I hope, if he's not dead. The only way to end this—for *me*, you understand?—is to go to the source and fuck up whoever started this. It sounds like that's Evalt. So if your plan is to kill him, I'm on board. You can trust me that far. Take it or leave it."

A heavy silence fell after that. Oskar wasn't trying to kill Callum. Yet. That might change at any moment. We all stood frozen, my heart sinking down to my feet.

"If you touch him," Oskar said at last, "if you hurt him, I'll kill you. No questions asked. I won't hesitate. You can take *that* or leave it."

"He promised not to hurt me," I said. I looked at Callum, and found him looking back at me, something dark in his unreadable eyes. "He promised not to hurt me," I said again, softly, wishing Callum would give me some sign he hadn't been lying to me. Hoping against hope for…I didn't even know what to hope for.

"Humans lie," Oskar snarled. "I think this one lies more than most."

"Yeah," Callum said, his voice a little hoarse. He was speaking to Oskar, but he didn't look away from me. I felt like he looked all the way through me, down to the pitiful, helpless part of me that longed to have faith in him. "I do. But I also keep my word."

"That's easy to say for a liar, but—"

Kaspar cut Oskar off with a sharp, "Hush!"

"What do you—"

"Be quiet!" Kaspar tilted his head to the side, listening.

Then I heard it too. The rushing, rhythmic sound of the beating of wings, followed by a chorus of harsh caws, growing nearer.

"Crows," Kaspar whispered. "They've found us."

Chapter Ten

Callum

Oskar snatched up his sword, shoved me out of the way, and flung the door open. "Linden, stay inside," he said, and ran out.

Kaspar went to his bag and started rummaging through it, muttering under his breath.

Linden stood frozen, his face completely white. Even his rosy lips had gone pale. He'd already looked like he was about to collapse.

Crows—and that begged for a fucking explanation, but what in this bizarre place didn't?—were the last straw, apparently. For a second, indecision took me over. Go to Linden? Try to comfort him? He'd wanted me to sleep with him, apparently, and fuck if I could figure out if that had been some kind of joke or not, but I doubted he wanted me to hug him.

I wasn't a hugger. Fuck. Did *I* want to hug *him*?

Yes, I fucking well did, and that shook me out of it.

I turned and followed Oskar outside. Deal with the immediate threat, even if that threat was some birds, and then deal with Linden later.

Maybe it was an avoidance tactic. Or maybe the crows breathed fire and Oskar needed backup. I could go either way on that at this point.

When I'd stepped out a few minutes before to find a convenient bush, the air had been chilly but the sky clear, a pure, too-blue blue that almost hurt my eyes. Now clouds were scudding in, moving faster than weather had any right to, and the sun had dimmed down to something like twilight.

Oskar stood with his feet braced apart and his head up, as if facing down an enemy, even though there wasn't anything there that I could see. He held his sword out in front of him in a two-handed grip. I drew my gun from its underarm holster, thumbed off the safety, and pulled the slide back. The familiar chunk and click gave me a little moment of normality.

That lasted for exactly a moment. The beating of wings and the caws of crows resolved into a group of birds coming in fast, skimming over the forest treetops. Eight or ten, it looked like. Oskar raised his sword higher. I moved into position next to him, and he shot me a suspicious glance.

"Kaspar looked busy," I said. "I don't have anything better to do than maybe shoot some crows."

Oskar grunted a laugh. "Don't shoot them. It won't do any good. They're not really birds."

Okay then. I kept my weapon at the ready anyway.

The crows swooped over the last of the trees at the edge of the little clearing that held the hunting lodge and settled in front of us with a great flurry of beating wings and loud cries. Dead leaves and dust swirled into the air in a choking cloud. Oskar and I stayed perfectly still, waiting. I wasn't used to my enemy being a flock of fucking birds, or not-really-birds, whatever, but an enemy was an enemy. It felt good to be standing my ground with someone else, something I hadn't done much of since I left the army ten years before.

Even if that someone else happened to be Oskar. I glanced sidelong at his sword, which wasn't even wobbling from the strain of holding it at that precise angle in midair. I could do a lot worse.

One of the crows strutted forward, leaving the other nine in a hostile, beady-eyed cluster.

I thought I'd started to get used to the weirdness of this place.

And then the crow opened its beak and said, "My master sees you, Oskar of Varnu. And he sees the one called the child of sunlight." The crow's voice creaked like a tree branch in a high wind, with a whispery undertone that sent a shudder down my spine. It felt like nails on a chalkboard.

"I see you, harbinger," Oskar replied grimly. "Speak."

"Lord Evalt summons the one called the child of sunlight to his home, there to meet his fate."

Oskar snorted. "No one's going anywhere on Lord Evalt's say-so. Tell him to go fuck himself."

I'd never in my life imagined that one day I'd hear a crow laugh. Cross that one off the bucket list, and fuck, but it was the creepiest sound I'd ever heard, a scratchy, hacking noise that had me itching to pull the trigger.

"The mother of the one called the child of sunlight will pay the price. And all who share her roof. Tomorrow at sunset, Oskar of Varnu."

Oskar cursed, and he lunged, swinging his sword in an arc that would've sliced the crow's head off. But the bird hopped backward, taking flight as it did, and all of its cohorts went with it.

Within seconds they'd shrunk to specks against the gray, gloomy sky, and moments later they were gone.

I lowered my gun and relaxed my grip; Oskar lowered his sword, sliding it back into its scabbard. For a minute or two we stood side by side, staring after the crows and thinking about the shitshow our day had suddenly become. I was, at least. Oskar probably had less processing to do regarding the talking bird.

"So I'm guessing Linden's the 'child of sunlight,' yeah?" Oskar nodded. I wondered if Linden had the name for any reason beyond how fucking sunny he was, but it didn't seem like the time

to ask Oskar why Linden was so pretty, like some high-school idiot with a crush. "Does Evalt already have his mother hostage, or
is he bluffing to get Linden out in the open? And if he knows
where we are, why isn't he already here? Why the crow bullshit?"

"This forest is under the protection of an ancient name, which
is why Kaspar brought us here. Lord Evalt isn't welcome here,
though he can send his messengers, as you've seen."

Well, that was as clear as fucking mud, but I guessed I got the
overall idea. "Okay. So he needs to lure us out of here, and Linden's mom is the obvious play."

"If I understand your odd phrasing correctly, yes, Linden's
mother is his most vulnerable point. If Evalt has her—and I think
he probably does, because he rarely bluffs—then Linden will think
nothing of sacrificing himself for her sake." Oskar paused, sighed,
and added, "Although even if Evalt doesn't have her hostage, Linden will go. He won't take the risk. And once Evalt knows where
Linden will be, he'll be easy pickings. There may be an ambush on
the road from here to there."

"That's what I'd do." I thought it over for a moment. "Is there
any reason for Linden to go at all? Someone needs to go. This asshole needs killing. But Linden's not going to be the one to do it, is
he?"

Oskar turned his head and fixed me with a penetrating stare,
the kind you'd get from a drill sergeant who knew you were up to
some kind of shady bullshit but wasn't quite sure of the details
yet.

"You don't know, do you." It wasn't a question any more
than mine had been; asking if Linden would be the one to pull the
trigger had been completely rhetorical. Of course he wouldn't. But
it seemed like I'd hit a nerve. "You have no idea why Evalt's so
intent on killing Linden, even though you were meant to be the
instrument of it," he said, with a not-so-pleasant emphasis.

I hid a wince. Yes, I was a mundane tool, thank you, he'd already made his opinion fucking clear.

But admit how little I really understood about what was going on, or not? Not much point in trying to pretend I knew more than I did, not now. I'd done that the night before, and nothing had come of it but more mistrust. And this morning—looking at Linden, standing there miserable and with all his natural light put out like someone had hit his dimmer switch, I couldn't lie. Not when he was so intent on trying to fudge the truth to his friends on my behalf as much as he could, trying to protect me from how much they'd naturally hate me for the way I'd come to meet Linden in the first place.

It was too much strain. He didn't owe me trying to make me more likeable. I *wasn't* fucking likeable. He needed to depend on his friends, not put himself at odds with them because of me.

So now they knew I'd been hired to kill Linden, and they might as well know I'd been full of shit about understanding the situation, too.

Maybe the only way to get information out of these people was to tell the truth myself. I didn't like to operate that way, opening myself up, so it surprised me what a fucking weight it lifted off my shoulders to just be—me. With all my faults.

"I have no fucking clue what's going on, Oskar. Someone in my world hired me to kill a guy who didn't look like someone anyone would want to kill. I dragged my feet, because no one in his right mind would want to murder Linden. Someone else tried to kill him, I reacted and iced the fucker. And then I ended up in a different fucking realm, with talking crows and bone-eating jelly monsters." Oskar was still looking at me, still with that hard, take-no-prisoners expression on his face. "You don't trust me, and you don't like me. But killing is something I'm really, really good at. So tell me what we're up against, give me the backstory so I don't fuck up because I don't know something, and I'll point my gun wherever you point your sword."

At last Oskar nodded. And then he held out his hand.

I took it. We both squeezed a little harder than strictly

necessary before letting go.

"I'll hold you to that," he said, and I nodded, one soldier to another. He sighed. "Lord Evalt has a seer, someone who can catch glimpses of the future. She's not a very good seer, mind you, but Evalt hangs on her every word. Evalt can't be killed by any weapon forged under the sun, but his power only makes him more paranoid. She predicted that someone she called the Light-Bearer would be the one to kill Evalt. Linden appears to fulfill her prophecy, because of the way the sun shone at his birth."

Maybe Oskar would've gone on, but that was more than fucking enough for me. "The sun. The fucking sun shone when he was born, I'm assuming during the day when the sun's supposed to goddamn shine, and this Evalt's been wanting to kill him ever since?" I wasn't shouting, but I wanted to. "The sun. Fuck, this place. And everyone thinks this makes *sense*? I can put up with the bone-eating things, okay, those I can shoot. The talking crows might be kind of cool if they weren't messengers of some evil ass-hole who wants to kill us all. But setting up *how* many fucking people to die? Hiring me to kill someone because the sun was out when he was born, like on a couple hundred other fucking days that year? *Fuck* that, Oskar!"

I broke off, breathing hard, and realized I'd been shouting af-ter all. The echo of my words rang from the trees around the lodge and hung in the air.

Oskar's lips twitched, and then he started to laugh. It grew from a belly chuckle to a full-on guffaw, and it broke my anger. Laughter bubbled up in me, too, until we were both cackling like idiots, the sound rolling around the clearing and lightening the air, somehow.

"What is *wrong* with you?"

We both spun, red-faced and gasping, to see Kaspar standing in the doorway of the lodge, his fists on his hips.

"Sorry," Oskar mumbled. "We were—" He glanced at me, and we exchanged a look of accord. There were times when the situation went so FUBAR there wasn't any choice but to just laugh your ass off. And anyone who'd ever fought in a war knew it.

"You were being idiots," Kaspar sniffed. "The crows are gone, I see. I should have had magic prepared in case, but I was too slow. I assume they've returned to their master."

Linden appeared behind Kaspar, peeking over his shoulder. "There's no reason I can't come out now," he complained. "Get out of my way."

"No," Oskar said. "There may be other spies. Stay inside, out of sight."

"What difference does it make? He knows where I am! And I want to know what message the crows brought!" He tried to shove his way past Kaspar, who shoved him back, and it devolved into the sort of squabbling match you'd see between siblings.

Six-year-old siblings.

"What's the plan?" I murmured to Oskar, quietly enough that Linden couldn't possibly hear me over the sound of his own protests. "Linden ought to stay here, but he won't stay willingly."

"I can't lie," Oskar said apologetically. I started to argue, but he held up a hand. "No, I truly can't lie. None of us can. It's part of our nature. Except for you."

I took a second to absorb that, thinking back over all the bizarro conversations I'd had with my three examples of people from this realm. In the labyrinth, Linden had told me he'd never lied to me, and I hadn't been able to refute it. Now I had some independent confirmation. This realm got weirder and weirder. "For guys who can't lie, you skirt the truth a whole fucking lot."

"It's our way," Oskar said. "But I'm being honest with you now, no sidestepping. I can't lie to Linden to make him stay behind. And you could."

Kaspar and Linden were still arguing, and it sounded like they'd moved on to bringing up childhood misbehavior on both sides to bolster their points. Christ. At least they were distracted.

And I needed them to stay that way, because I couldn't make

up my mind. Leaving Linden behind had a lot of advantages, mainly the whole 'Linden not being available for Evalt to murder' thing, with a side of 'not having to protect him while I watched my own back.' But could I lie to him about something so important? Yes, on balance. Would it work, though?

"I don't think there's anything I can say to him that'll keep him here. Even if we leave out anything about his mom. Even if we tell him Evalt's summoned him to a meeting place somewhere else. He won't stay behind, because he won't let us go off to maybe die for him. Won't let you do that, anyway. If he had any sense, he'd let me do it no problem."

Oskar nodded, giving me a grunt of agreement. Fuck, but it was refreshing to talk to someone who didn't see the point in sugar-coating anything.

"He doesn't have any sense," Oskar said after a second. "We'd have to compel him somehow. I'd be willing to do that, but we'd need Kaspar's help, and he wouldn't agree. He'd say Linden wasn't a child and shouldn't be treated like one."

Linden might be arguing like one right at that moment, but then again, so was Kaspar. I took the opportunity to stare my fill. Linden wasn't childlike. If he had been, I wouldn't have been getting hard thinking about him wanting me to keep him warm at night.

Fuck.

But with his soft mouth and wide blue eyes and slender, graceful everything, he *was* delicate. Fragile, even, compared to me or Oskar. Of course, I'd seen monster trucks that were fragile compared to Oskar—but I wasn't a fair comparison either. I'd been shot three times, stabbed more often than I'd bothered to keep track of, concussed, thrown out of a helicopter, and beaten up enough that it didn't bother me anymore. And here I was, still alive and pissed off.

No, not a fair comparison.

Still. He wasn't *weak*. I didn't need any more proof of that than the fact he'd insist on going with us if he knew what was up, and I didn't doubt that for a second. He was a man, not a kid, and he had the right to go die in the effort to save his own mother's life if he fucking well wanted to. I didn't have to like it. I just had to accept it.

"I'm not lying to him about this. Sorry. No can do."

Oskar looked at me long and hard, and finally nodded slowly. "For the record, I disagree with that decision."

"Sure you do. But you're relieved anyway. You don't have to decide, and you know if you did it'd be wrong."

Oskar barked a laugh. "Fair enough. All right. Are we going to draw straws for which of us has to tell him what the crow said?"

"Absolutely not," I said. "You've known him longer. This one's all yours."

"Fuck you," Oskar sighed resignedly, and we headed back to the lodge to break up the fight and face the music.

Chapter Eleven

Linden

We'd marched for nearly six hours, and I'd begun to wish I'd spent more time walking during my exile to the human realm. My legs burned, my back ached, and I couldn't feel my feet. That last might've been a good thing if it hadn't meant I kept stumbling over every root and rock.

In front of me, Oskar strode ahead like he'd just popped out of a featherbed. Beside me, Kaspar muttered low-voiced complaints but went on gamely enough. And behind me—well, I couldn't see what Callum was doing, but I'd have been willing to bet he hadn't flagged, and that his expression hadn't changed in the slightest from the hard, focused look he'd had ever since he and Oskar came inside and told me my mother would die the following day if we didn't walk into a trap.

I knew I should've been afraid, anxious, overwhelmed with worry and grief.

But I wasn't. I couldn't feel anything. My peaceful, rural home, with its low stone walls separating sheep pastures from farmland, its deep-green hedgerows and pale-green meadows, its brilliant, many-hued roses and orchards of apples and apricots...Lord Evalt was there now, his troops churning the gardens to mud with their heavy boots and filling Lady Lisandra's quiet halls with harsh laughter and curses.

It wasn't real. It couldn't be real, because I simply couldn't make it more than a nightmare.

My mother, forced to kneel before Lord Evalt, weeping.

Or perhaps she wouldn't weep. Perhaps she'd hold her head up and spit in his face. She'd always been braver than I had.

My numbness might've passed for bravery if someone watching didn't know any better. I put one stumbling foot in front of the other, and I wasn't crying or pleading or storming with rage. But I couldn't feel.

I needed to feel, or the pressure building up behind my eyes might go off all at once and tear me to pieces.

One foot in front of the other. It went on and on. We had to hurry. The lodge had been a full three days' hike from home, when we'd had all the time in the world to enjoy the quiet forest paths and their fragrance of pine and running water and sunshine on the branches above us. Now we had less than two days. We'd make it, but it meant keeping up a pace that felt brutal after the events of the days before.

And then it stopped, and I collided with Oskar's broad back, my chin knocking painfully into the hard leather of his pauldron.

"Is something wrong?" Callum asked quietly from right behind me. He'd stopped without running into me, of course.

"I heard something," Oskar said, even more quietly. "I'll scout ahead. Wait here. Kaspar, light out."

Kaspar whispered a word to his staff, which went out instantly. A little frisson of fear raised the hair on the back of my neck. Oskar wasn't one to jump at shadows, and I could feel Callum's tension, a sudden thrumming hardness in the air. Anger joined the fear. Did they know something I didn't? Had they held something back?

For someone so bulky, Oskar could be shockingly stealthy, and he disappeared between the trees without so much as a snapped twig or a rustle of the dry leaves beneath his feet. I strained my eyes, trying to watch his progress, but I couldn't see anything. The moon hung high and nearly full, but the little shafts of light filtering through the branches above us weren't enough to make out more than vague shapes.

Callum tried to slip past me, and I grabbed his arm. "Where do you think you're going?" I hissed.

"Watching Oskar's six," he muttered, and pulled free, jogging after Oskar. He wasn't quite as silent, but very close. Once he'd vanished too, I felt incredibly lost and lonely and alone, even with Kaspar beside me.

I huddled closer to him, and I waited.

Callum

I couldn't see Oskar ahead of me, but I didn't need to. All my instincts were on full alert, and we weren't alone in these woods. I'd heard something too. A faint jingle and the stamp of feet.

The others hadn't been able to tell me precisely when we'd leave the dodgy protection of the forest's 'ancient name,' whatever the fuck that meant—at least in terms of miles, though they'd mentioned some landmarks that also meant nothing to me. Despite my skepticism, though, I'd felt a difference a few miles back.

The air had changed. That was the best way I could describe it, and it made me really fucking uncomfortable to acknowledge that what I'd felt was magic.

So I knew that if we were going to get ambushed, it'd be somewhere here. They could figure out as well as we could how long it'd take to walk to Linden's home, and set up somewhere we'd be passing at night, when we were already tired, and outside the other forest's invisible boundary.

A moment later, I didn't even need to try to follow Oskar's trail. A shout rang out, followed by the clash of metal on metal. I already had the Beretta in my hand, and I cocked it as I ran, hoping Linden and Kaspar had the sense to say out of it.

The trees thinned, and through them I caught a glimpse of a clearing full of sword-wielding men bathed in moonlight, a cluster of horses at the other side, and Oskar's bulky figure whirling in the middle of it. His sword reflected the moon like a mirror, throwing sparks of white in all directions. More shouts filled the air, and a cry of pain as Oskar's sword found a target. The soldiers swarming around Oskar wore black leather armor, but the metal studs in the leather caught the moonlight and made them easy fucking targets. It could be a challenge in combat sometimes to only hit the enemy, but in this case, I only had one friendly to miss. The silver lining to being outnumbered as fuck—twelve to two as far as I could tell.

I ducked behind a fallen trunk, getting a little bit of cover just in case they had any ranged weapons, and took aim at the asshole right behind Oskar, dead center of mass. A head shot would've been better; at this range studded boiled leather might slow down an FMJ round enough to matter. And as soon as I fired, they'd know they had company and be on me like they were on Oskar…not to mention, I didn't have unlimited ammo. But in uncertain lighting and at this range, I didn't have much choice, either.

The fucker paused in place, raising his sword, and I paused too, wishing I had my M24. But when I pulled the trigger, the bullet hit dead on, and he stumbled and went down. Half the men in the clearing spun to stare, crying out in a language I didn't understand—but I didn't need to. *What the ever-loving fuck was that* translated just fine. I grinned and took aim again. Double-tap to the chest, and another one down. And then a third shot, a miss, but my fourth shot hit its target, the ringing in my ears drowning out the screams. The rest had scattered like roaches, taking cover or racing to the side of the clearing to try to flank me. The third guy I'd hit had fallen to his knees, so I put another one through him before I jumped out of my crouch to get a better position. Oskar didn't stop, cutting down two more of his opponents while I fired on the others.

That left seven, two to my right and two to my left, with the other three still taking cover or dodging Oskar. I put two more rounds into the clearing in the direction of one of the guys who'd crouched behind a tree stump and then dodged back, glancing back and forth to try to get a bead on the four coming my way.

There, to the right. One of them came out from behind a tree, and I fired twice, winging him in the shoulder as far as I could tell. A shout to my left and the clash of metal on metal suggested Oskar had followed those two.

Four bullets left in the Beretta. Switch guns? Not yet. Fuck it. That was enough for the wounded one and his buddy. I went straight for them, and the one I hadn't hit yet jumped out from behind a tree, sword swinging, closer than I thought he'd gotten. Two shots to the chest took him almost down, but he lunged. I put another round between his eyes.

The other guy came at me, blood running down his arm, and swung close enough to part my hair. I ducked, cursing, and got my last shot off. It hit him in the leg, and he went down too.

I shoved my useless weapon back in my shoulder holster and pulled the Sig out of my waistband, and ran back toward Oskar to help him out with his share.

It wasn't necessary. I found him next to two corpses, leaning against a tree and favoring his left leg, breathing hard, with blood spattered all over his face. He still had his sword up and ready, though.

"I'll do a circle of the clearing and make sure they're all down, but I think that's all," I said. "You okay?"

Oskar nodded, and then he grinned at me, his teeth glinting. "You're a worthy comrade, Callum."

"Sit down before you fall down," I said, and hit him in the shoulder as I passed him. His laughter followed me back to the clearing.

I did a careful circuit, keeping my Sig up and ready, with my weird magical flashlight aimed with it. Nothing came out from the trees. The horses tethered at the edge of the clearing whinnied and stamped, and I gave them a wide berth, even though I knew I'd probably end up on one once we got moving again. Horses weren't my thing, ditto anything else that needed to be fed and humored. I'd grown up in central LA and hadn't seen a horse in real life until I deployed the first time. My footsteps sounded loud as hell now that the battle was over. A few groans echoed out of the clearing, and I'd deal with the source of those next, but it didn't sound like anyone still alive would be going anywhere.

Voices behind me made me turn and listen. Linden and Kaspar, and beneath their voices, Oskar's rumble. They'd caught up with him, then.

A moment later, Kaspar came jogging after me, the light on his staff bobbing.

"Oskar says there may be some survivors," he said as he approached. "I'll take care of that. I'll try to use magic to question them, but I may simply have to kill them."

His tone didn't give me much confidence. Kaspar sounded like a man trying to convince himself more than me. False bravado didn't help anyone.

"*We'll* take care of that," I corrected him, making a mental note to do any killing myself. He nodded, biting his lip and looking relieved. "Linden's staying with Oskar?" He nodded again, and I turned to head into the clearing with some relief of my own. Dealing with the temporary survivors wouldn't be pretty, and it wasn't something Linden needed to see.

It didn't take long. Only two of Lord Evalt's men had lived long enough for us to question, and one of those died within a minute. The other cursed, and spat, and refused to answer, and Kaspar muttered spells and waved his hands without any effect.

At last he stood, shaking his head. We weren't getting any information out of him.

I didn't want to waste another bullet, so I picked up a discarded sword and put it through the soldier's neck. Quick and clean. Kaspar flinched at the sound of it.

"Thank you," he said quietly. "I've never killed anyone. I know I could if I had to, but…"

I didn't make him finish the thought. "Not wanting to kill anyone isn't a character flaw." I dropped the bloodstained sword to the grass next to the body and surveyed the clearing. It looked like a slaughterhouse. "I have enough blood on my hands already. It doesn't matter at this point."

"It always matters," Kaspar said. Then he added, "But I'm glad you're on our side."

There didn't seem to be much to add to that; we turned and headed back to find Linden and Oskar. I spent the short walk mulling over whether Kaspar had meant that as a compliment or not. I was pretty sure he hadn't, and I couldn't explain why it made me feel so shitty. I'd never cared before.

Fuck it. There were wounds to treat and horses to steal and a sorcerer to fucking kill with extreme prejudice, and I had better things to do than navel-gaze.

Chapter Twelve

Linden

When the sound of the fight finally faded into a chilling silence, I gave in to impulse at last and ran after Oskar and Callum as if all of Lord Evalt's minions were on my heels—instead of right in front of me, waiting for me to fall into their clutches.

I'd wanted to follow them at once, but Kaspar's restraining hands on my arms had held me in place long enough for some common sense to take over my panic. Callum and Oskar were fighting because of me, maybe dying because of me. But I'd be useless to them, with my nonexistent skills with a weapon.

When I reached Oskar, the fight was clearly over. I found him leaned up against a tree, supporting his other side with his sword point-down in the forest mould. Blood trickled down his face and ran in rivulets over one of his legs. Kaspar skidded to a halt beside me, cursing in his turn.

I spun on him. "This is why you should've let me go!" I cried, a little unfairly. I turned back, glancing around wildly. "Where's Callum? Oskar, *where is he*?"

"He's fine, not a scratch I don't think. Those human weapons are wonderful. And put a cork in it, Linden," Oskar growled. "You'd have died in the first five seconds. You're not even armed, and it wouldn't do you much good if you were. I tried to teach you and Kaspar to fight, remember? It didn't take."

That was a massive understatement, and exactly what I'd told myself a few minutes before—but I was too angry and too weak with relief to admit it or to argue coherently. "That doesn't matter! You—*fuck* you, Oskar! Sit down and let me look at your wounds. I need you whole again so I won't feel guilty when I strangle you."

Callum was alive. Oskar was alive. The words repeated and repeated in my mind, though I wouldn't quite believe it until I saw Callum for myself. I'd heard the screams, and gunshot after gunshot, each one shredding my nerves all over again no matter how quickly they came in succession. When the gun went silent it was worse.

But they were alive, and I'd cowered behind them like a useless idiot, and now I could at least tend to Oskar's leg.

He slid to the ground and stretched out his wounded leg, and I started in on tearing the fabric of his trousers back from the sword-cut so I could get a better look at it. I vaguely heard Oskar telling Kaspar to go and try to question anyone left alive, and then Kaspar was off, leaving me alone with Oskar.

He grunted in discomfort as I prodded the cut in his thigh. It was moderately deep, but just in the muscle of his leg, far enough from any arteries for comfort. I poked at it again, not bothering to be gentle.

"Don't take it out on me," he grumbled. "You knew it'd be like this. You're not a soldier. There's no shame in it. Neither is Kaspar. There wouldn't be any shame in it even if he *was* a soldier too."

I realized my cheeks were hot and wet, and that tears had been streaming down unchecked. I hadn't even noticed. "Kaspar's magic is strong enough to be useful. I'm not good for anything. I'm worthless."

"We wouldn't be risking our lives for you if you were

worthless," Oskar snapped. "You're worth a lot to me. And Kaspar."

I couldn't help noticing he'd left Callum off the list, and my chest clenched.

No, I had to squelch that feeling. Callum had his own reasons for being here, for fighting Lord Evalt. They didn't have much to do with me, even if he'd landed in this mess indirectly because of me. Wishing otherwise was neither fair nor helpful.

Kaspar had dropped his satchel next to us, and I rummaged through it for something clean to bind the wound with. And if I knew him, there'd be some kind of healing salve in there, too. I might even have made it for him.

Seeming to read my mind, Oskar said, "If Kaspar has anything in there that'll close my wound and keep it clean, it'll be because of you and your recipes. That's far from useless. And your worth isn't dependent on how useful you are, anyway." He paused. "Although if you could hurry up and find it and stop poking me on purpose, I'd like you a lot more than I do right now."

I glanced up at him through my lashes and found him smiling at me, and it went a long way to soothing the ache in my chest. Oskar had always been like a brother to me, solid and dependable and loving. My life wasn't worth the sacrifice of his, and I'd do my best, his counter-efforts aside, to prevent that from happening.

But it mattered that he didn't agree with me. Maybe that was all the worth I needed to have in the world: my friendship giving someone as strong, honorable, and decent as Oskar enough joy that he'd be willing to sacrifice himself for me.

I finished salving and binding his leg in silence, trying to let that hard lump in my chest dissolve a little as I worked.

Footsteps and low voices reached my ears as I finished. Callum and Kaspar. I kept my head down. Oskar and Kaspar knew me and my limitations, and my talents, too, such as they were. To Callum, I wasn't anything special. Just dead weight who couldn't hold his own in a fight. A target, whether Evalt's or Callum's. A man like Callum would value the ability to fight more than anything, wouldn't he? Despite their rocky start, he and Oskar had clearly learned to admire and respect one another. Maybe Callum preferred men like Oskar. They certainly had infinitely more in common, and who wouldn't respect Oskar more than they respected me?

Kaspar dropped down next to Oskar and put a hand on his shoulder, giving it a squeeze. He started a low-voiced explanation of what they'd learned from the wounded enemy. It sounded like not much at all, and my mood sank even lower.

And then Callum crouched next to me, not Oskar, so close that our shoulders brushed.

"Are you all right?" he asked in English, his voice as low as Kaspar's. "I'm glad you stayed back. Thank you."

It meant something that he'd spoken in a language he knew my friends couldn't understand, that he wanted to speak just to me. But my temper flared, fed by all the self-doubt I'd been marinating in while I bound up Oskar's wound. "For not getting in your way?" I asked bitterly. "This is my fight. I should've been fighting with you."

He stayed silent for a moment. "Yeah, you'd have been in the way, but not how you mean."

I sniffed, and realized in horror that I sounded exactly like my mother. "There's only one way you could mean that." I was so tired, so very, miserably tired. I'd been crouching too, but I gave up and slumped down onto the ground. A pebble poked me in the ass. Typical.

Callum sighed. "They were after you, Linden. If they'd seen you, they'd have gone for their primary target. And then you'd have been in my sights every time I tried to take a shot. In the dark, in unfamiliar terrain, with limited ammunition…you'd have been in the way, yeah. But so was Oskar, to an extent. If you're the objective, it makes more sense to keep you in the background."

Oskar looked up at the sound of his name. "If you're going to talk shit about me, have the courtesy to do it in a language I understand," he said.

Callum replied in our language, something teasing about how he'd never know enough languages to adequately describe how ugly Oskar was, but I barely paid attention. My mind whirled, trying to take in what Callum had said. He hadn't sounded angry at all—or contemptuous, which would've been more what I'd have expected.

It was simply practical. I wasn't one of Callum's targets, so it made it easier to have me out of the way of his bullets.

And I'd have been lying if I pretended to myself that Callum wanting to protect me didn't make me feel better.

Oskar started to insist he could walk, and we all levered ourselves off the ground, brushing off dirt and leaves. The night felt like it had already stretched on forever, an endless expanse of exhaustion and fear, with more yet to come. I wanted to curl up in a cozy bed and sleep for a week. I wanted my mother, safe and sound. I wanted some comfort, something, anything.

"We'll choose some of the horses to take, and set the others free," Kaspar said. "Go and get some sleep."

I'd been staring into the trees, lost in thought, and it took me a moment to realize he expected an answer. "I can help with the horses."

Kaspar shook his head. "Two of us will be enough. Oskar needs to choose a horse that can bear him, but any of them can carry you. And I want to go through the saddlebags and see if there's anything useful."

"We'll find somewhere to get some shut-eye," Callum said. "Over there." He gestured to the left. "Upwind from the clearing. I'll wake up at dawn, guaranteed."

We were almost certainly going to die the following day. And now Callum was going to lead me into the woods, alone...that gave me ideas. Probably very bad ideas. But as soon as they'd taken root in my mind, they grew and grew despite my attempts to stifle them. I leaned down and snatched up the jar of salve I'd used for Oskar's leg, stuffing it into my pocket as quickly as I could. And then I pulled Kaspar aside as Callum and Oskar exchanged a few words about the plan for the morning.

"Sleep somewhere else," I whispered.

Kaspar stared at me. "You're joking."

"Sleep. Somewhere. Else. Sit on Oskar if you need to." I couldn't be certain in the dim light, but Kaspar...blushed? Yes, he *was* blushing, his cheekbones stained dark like wine. And that...oh, I couldn't even begin to tackle that at the moment. They were like brothers too, weren't they? Had the implication simply embarrassed him? "Anyway, stay away until dawn."

Kaspar gave me another exasperated look, but Oskar pulled him away, leaving Callum and me standing alone in the filtered moonlight, listening to their footsteps fading into nothing. Callum's face held that same neutral, closed expression he'd worn all day, without a trace of emotion. If I hadn't known he'd killed half a dozen men an hour before, I'd never have been able to tell.

"Doesn't it bother you?" The words slipped out before I could restrain them. I couldn't imagine killing and simply shrugging and walking away. And Callum...how could he be so gentle sometimes, but so brutal in a fight? "Spending so much of your life bringing death."

Something passed across Callum's hard face, and he couldn't quite meet my eyes, looking over my shoulder. "No." A pause. "Sometimes. But sometimes it's—we should get some rest."

"Sometimes it's what?" I wasn't going to let this go. He'd come so close to speaking to me like a person, not an adversary or an inconvenience or an oddity. I wanted him. I could admit that to myself, here in the near-dark with my own death looming so close I couldn't even get a full picture of it, since it filled all my senses. But I didn't know if I could go through with trying to get what I wanted if I didn't know Callum saw *me*, Linden. If I didn't know he could give me some little bit of himself.

The silence stretched. "Sometimes it's fun," he said at last in a rush, almost under his breath.

I blinked at him. I knew Oskar enjoyed a good fight, and that wasn't alien to me. But the killing itself? "Fun?"

Callum met my eyes at last. "I had this one job—come on, let's find a place to sleep, and I'll tell you on the way." I nodded and we set off through the trees. "There was this nice suburban housewife who hired me. I still don't know how she found me. I think her cousin was an ex-con, and he knew someone—anyway. Somehow she got in touch. She offered me fifty thousand dollars to kill her neighbor. Said she'd tried calling the cops over and over again, but they couldn't do anything, and she was at her wits' end, because he kept waking up her kids. So, okay, weird, and fifty grand isn't usually enough, but she—okay, this is really embarrassing."

I glanced up at him. "More embarrassing than admitting killing people is fun?"

Callum frowned and looked at me too, and for a second our gazes caught and held. His eyes glinted, catching a stray shaft of moonlight. "I'm not embarrassed about that. It's just the truth. I thought you people were all about telling the truth no matter what."

"We're as dishonest as humans," I said. "We can't lie directly. But we find ways around it."

"Yeah, I've noticed." He sighed. "All right, so here's the embarrassing part. She used her mom voice on me."

"Her—oh, you can't be serious." I started to laugh, helpless to stop it. It had taken me a moment to understand the idiom, but...yes, some concepts were universal. I remembered my mother shouting at me from the kitchen door to stop ruining her herb garden playing too roughly with Oskar, and fought off a wave of sadness. My laughter died away.

"Sorry," Callum said awkwardly. "I didn't mean to—you know we'll get there in time, right? She'll be all right. I promise."

"You can't promise that. What happened to telling me the truth?"

Callum was so close, close enough that I could see the slight tic in his jaw as he stared me down. Our heights almost matched. Near enough, anyway, that he could've kissed me without having to do more than tilt his head.

Or I could kiss him. I never minded being the instigator, although Callum seemed like a man who'd want to be in control.

And I wouldn't mind that, either. Far from it.

"I'm promising to do my best, then, I guess," he said. "That's all I can offer you."

"That's more than I could ask for." I couldn't stop looking away from his mouth. That pressure from earlier had returned, more insistently this time. Something had to give way, or I'd run screaming into the woods. I could hardly hold still, even though I was simultaneously tired enough to collapse. My head felt three times its size, filled to bursting with everything I still couldn't feel properly. "Callum." It came out a hoarse whisper. "Callum, I need…"

He laughed, quick and harsh. "Yeah. One battle down, another battle tomorrow. I know what you need. That's the same in every realm."

Before I could respond, his hands were on my waist, and he pushed, walking me backward until I hit a tree. And then his mouth covered mine, hard and determined.

Chapter Thirteen

Linden

I hadn't been kissed in a long time, and I couldn't remember being kissed like this at all. Callum devoured me, his fingers digging into my hips and his mouth claiming mine. I caught fistfuls of his jacket and dragged him closer. He ground his hips against me, his cock hardening as he thrust.

Mine rose desperately to meet it. All that thrumming tension in my body came to the surface, demanding more kisses, more friction, *more*. Callum might not be much taller, but he outweighed me by enough to have me trapped against the tree, enough that I knew if he was on top of me I'd be pinned and helpless.

I moaned into his mouth, tangling my tongue with his and wrapping my arms around his back. Callum's stubble scratched against my lips, rubbing them raw and swollen. I wanted more of that. I wanted him to mark me. If I died tomorrow, I wanted to be so well-used and thoroughly fucked that I could think of that, instead of what I faced.

Callum tore his mouth away and bit at my throat, hot and stinging and perfect. I tipped my head back. Tree branches swam above me, blurry in my half-focused vision. Callum panted against my skin. One of his hands held me still at my waist, while the other found its way around my back, sliding down into my jeans, the fingers teasing lower.

"Yes," I gasped. "Yes, *that*."

"We don't have anything," he said against my neck. But he didn't stop working his hand down, his middle finger teasing my crease and the rest of his hand massaging my cheeks.

I let go of him and shoved him back so I could get a hand into my pocket. Callum resisted, pushing me back against the tree. "I have—mmph," I said as he took my mouth again. My lips parted for him without resistance. I couldn't help it. "I have—in my pocket."

Callum pulled back enough to stare at me. He looked surprisingly wrecked, his own lips shiny and his cheeks flushed, his dark eyes a little glazed. "You brought lube. To a forest?"

I finally managed to get the little jar out of my pocket and waved it at him. "Not lube, technically. But it's slippery. And it's safe for internal use."

Callum blinked at me, and then a wide, mischievous grin spread over his face. He had such grim features usually. Smiling like that, he took my breath away—or what I had left after that last spate of kisses.

"We should find somewhere to lie down, then—"

"No," I said. "Here. Against the tree. Right here. And don't even try to be gentle with me."

Callum's eyebrows shot up, and he leaned in, teasing my mouth with his, brushing back and forth over my swollen, tingling flesh and making me squirm. "So demanding," he muttered. "Be fucking careful what you ask for." He thrust his hips again, hard, and his cock felt like iron.

"I want something else first," I whispered, and pushed him back enough that I could drop down on my knees. He had to pull his hand out of my pants, and I wanted it back.

But I wanted this more. I wanted to feel him forcing my mouth open, to imagine what it'd feel like between my legs, to work myself up to such a fever of impatience that I'd be begging him to fuck me without mercy.

"Fuck," Callum said. "You don't have to." But he was already tearing at the button of his jeans.

My mouth watered as he jerked his fly open and pulled out his cock, shifting his feet to make it possible to set it free of the constriction of his clothes. He had more than enough inches to fill my mouth and thrust down my throat, and later…he'd make me scream. Hopefully he'd cover my mouth, or Oskar might come running and we'd all regret it.

I leaned in and licked.

Callum

Linden's tongue flicked over the head of my cock, the contrast between the hot sweetness of his mouth and the cold evening air enough to make me shudder.

Fuck, *fuck* but it'd been a long time since I had someone's mouth on me.

Before I'd even come to terms with his tongue, Linden took me fully into his mouth, swallowing me down and into his throat like he'd been practicing every day for years. And wasn't that a fucking thought. He dug his fingers into my hips and looked up at me, his blue eyes wide and dark, filled with something I couldn't name.

His fingers curled, pressing into me harder. Slowly, I moved my own hand and laid it on his throat. Linden swallowed around my cock, moaning, the vibrations traveling all the way through my cock and my balls and up my spine.

I squeezed him, just enough pressure to constrict what airway he had left with my dick filling him up. Linden started to suck like his life depended on it, his head bobbing and his tongue swirling around me over and over, laving every inch of me.

I wasn't going to fucking keep it together. Not with his hot, eager mouth surrounding me, not with his slender throat flexing under my hand, the skin soft and tender.

Did he know how much I could hurt him, if I wanted to? Yeah, I was pretty sure he did, and he was getting off on it. So was I.

I squeezed a little harder. He pulled off enough to take a breath, panting and whimpering, and the moonlight struck pale glints off the moisture at the corners of his eyes.

With one hand still on his throat, I dared to do what I'd been wanting to for—honestly since I saw him in the coffee shop the first time. I wrapped my other hand in that dandelion-silk hair, feeling the delicate strands catch on my callused fingers, and held his head in place.

My first thrust made him grip onto my hips so hard it hurt, and then he opened his throat, gazed up at me, and fucking took it.

I fucked his mouth hard, every motion driving deeper into the hot constriction of his throat. He swallowed around me frantically, and I pulled back enough to let him get a breath before I plunged back in again. My whole body drew tight, teetering on the edge.

I pulled out of his mouth abruptly, gasping when my spit-slick cock hit the cold air.

"I want it," Linden said, his voice a shattered, wrecked rasp. God, I wanted to come on his pretty face while he talked to me like that, told me how much he wanted me to mess him up. "Don't stop."

But what he'd already offered me would be even better. "Get up and turn around." My own voice wasn't much smoother, even though I hadn't had eight thick inches forced into my throat. "Pants down, and give me that jar."

Linden flailed as he tried to get up, and I let go of his neck and his hair with regret to pull him to his feet. For a moment, he slumped against me, breathing hard, and I nuzzled the side of his head. He still smelled like fresh spring greenery, even after a couple of days of hiking and sleeping in the hunting lodge. We'd stopped for a few minutes that afternoon and washed up in a stream, thank God, or I wouldn't have felt all right about putting my dick in his mouth, but still.

I didn't want to let him go, but my cock throbbed insistently, wanting to know why the fuck I'd stopped the blowjob if I wasn't going to give it something better.

"Against the tree," I murmured in his ear, and I slid my hands down to fondle his ass. He shivered, and I gave another hard squeeze. He didn't have much ass, but what he did have fit perfectly in my hands. I pulled those small globes apart and pressed them together again, loving the way he rutted up against me and whispered something I couldn't quite catch in his own language, sounding broken and desperate.

He didn't seem inclined or able to move, so I turned him around and pressed him against the tree, tugging his hips out so that his ass was canted at the right angle. He worked his jeans open and shoved them down until they got stuck right above his knees.

I took a second to stare. His skin was just as smooth and pale there as everywhere else, and he glowed in the dimness of the forest. Fuck, but he looked unreal like that, offering himself up, ass out and begging to be fucked. Or licked, or spanked...my palm itched to smack one perfect, round cheek and then the other, but now wasn't the time. I'd gotten a little out of control, and I wouldn't hold back on fucking him, but he was so high on adrenaline and pre-battle jitters and anxiety and the need to feel something, anything else that he wouldn't stop me if I pushed right past what he could take, or wanted to take.

There wouldn't be a next time, but I couldn't think about that.

Take what I could get, and try to forget about it by morning. That'd worked for me before, and it had to be enough now.

This already went so far past what I deserved, anyway.

I stepped up behind him, letting my cock kiss the crease of

his ass. God, I wanted to thrust right in, but…not yet. "Where's the jar?"

"Sorry," Linden gasped. "On the ground."

I grabbed it and yanked the stopper out, letting that fall back down. It'd be a mess, and hopefully none of us would need it again…and if we did, it'd be too little too late, anyway. Tomorrow we'd either live or die, and that was that.

Linden moaned as I pushed two slicked fingers between his cheeks and brushed my fingertips over his hole. It'd been a while since I fucked a guy, but muscle memory took over and I probed him open, careful not to go too fast.

And it wasn't nearly fast enough for him. He shoved his ass back onto my fingers. "You won't break me," he gritted out.

In reply, I shoved my fingers deeper and twisted my hand, finding his prostate and pushing on it without mercy.

Linden howled, writhing around my hand. I pegged him hard, not letting up at all, the tightness of his body clenching around me driving me nearly as wild as it was making him.

Enough. Even if he could take more, I couldn't.

I slicked up my cock and leaned over his back, letting the head push against his hole. I wasn't going to go easy on him, because message fucking received, but I *was* going to make him ask me first before I gave it to him. My hand found its way around his throat again. They fit so perfectly, my big hand, so used to doing violence, and his slim neck, so breakable. I could kill him in a few different ways within seconds in this position. He wouldn't even be able to scream.

And he trusted me. He'd made himself as vulnerable to me as he could possibly get.

I needed to hear him tell me how much he wanted it.

"How hard do you want me to fuck you, Linden?"

"How hard can you fuck me?" He was aiming for bravado, I thought, but that little hitch in his voice gave him away.

I leaned in and pressed a line of kisses down the back of his neck, hating the fabric of his shirt cutting me off from going lower. I nudged with my cock until the head pressed into him. Just the tip, but it made us both gasp as his body tightened around me.

"I guess you'll find out, won't you?"

"Oh," he said, and shivered. "Yes, please."

Well, I could be a gentleman when someone asked nicely. I thrust the whole length of my cock inside him in one go.

Linden's entire body went rigid, and he let out a gasp that could've been a voiceless scream. I pulled out slowly, savoring the drag of friction, savoring his trembling anticipation even more, and slammed back into him as hard as I could.

He did scream then. I slid my hand up and clapped it over his mouth, stifling the tail end of it. His tongue slid against my palm and I fucked into him even harder than I'd meant to, making his feet skid in the loose leaves and dirt.

Fuck it. He'd wanted me to show him what I'd got, so I fucking would.

I wrapped the other arm around his waist to pin him in place, and then I pounded him into the next fucking realm.

Sweat trickled down my spine even in the chill, and his half-suppressed cries and my harsh panting breaths filled the air. Nothing mattered. Not the fight that night, not the fight to come, not Jesse's fate, not the fact that I'd probably never go home.

Nothing mattered but Linden's heat surrounding me and the way his slim body twisted and bucked in my hold. Nothing mattered but getting him off in a way he'd never forget.

I bent my knees enough to change the angle of my thrusts, and he let out another scream, so I knew I had it.

A few more thrusts like that, and he shook against me. His come spattered my arm. I let myself go, closing my eyes and racing to the finish, spilling inside him in pulse after pulse that nearly turned me inside out.

I slumped over his back, my hand falling away from his mouth. I let it settle on his hip, absently massaging the jut of the bone and the softness of his skin. His hip fit just right in my hand, too. Every part of him seemed to. He fit *me*, in some bizarrely unlikely way, this man from another fucking world who'd never killed anyone and made magic hot chocolate. I didn't want to let him go.

"I'm going to fall down," Linden mumbled.

Except for that. I'd worn myself out, too, and if I let him take my weight we'd both end up flat on the ground.

Pulling out felt like leaving home, but I managed. So much for washing up in that stream earlier. Linden was going to be sticky for a while. When I slowly let him go, making sure he could hold himself up, and I saw my come slicking the insides of his thighs—yeah, I couldn't even feel guilty about it. He looked so fucking hot like that, all messed up and wet. I did feel a little bad when I got my own pants fastened up and then started to help him pull up his, realizing that we didn't have anything to clean him off with. He really was going to be sticky.

Linden didn't seem to care, levering himself off the tree and buttoning his jeans without comment. I'd have put money on feeling awkward as hell in the aftermath, but I didn't. It was a true afterglow. Slow and lazy and peaceful, with the quiet between us feeling more like the presence of something easy than the absence of anything to say.

I wrapped my arm around him and pulled him close, because fuck it. Why not. And then I led him through the forest until we found a sheltered, more-or-less flat spot between several trees.

Linden wobbled on his feet, barely keeping himself up even leaning against me. And it was cold. Not much comfort to be found, but I'd had worse. I maneuvered him down onto the ground, stripped my jacket, shrugged out of my shoulder holster, and unclipped my IWB. I pulled the Sig out of the latter and set it and the flashlight in easy reach.

Getting settled on my back sucked, since the damp chill of the ground went right through my shirt and straight into my bones, but it sucked a lot less when Linden curled up next to me, putting his head on my shoulder and his arm over my waist without any prompting. His silky hair drifted up to tickle my chin and nose. I got my jacket draped over the both of us, with my arm under it to hold him close. A blanket would've been nice, but the only one we'd brought with us from the cabin had stayed with Kaspar—and the jacket was better than nothing.

Having Linden pressed against me all warm and soft felt better than just about anything.

I stared up at the tiny bit of sky I could see, navy blue and peppered with stars, crisscrossed with the invisible black of branches. The stars seemed closer and brighter here, although how could they be? Although—fuck, I'd been assuming we were on Earth. And that wasn't necessarily true.

"You never finished telling me about the housewife who wanted her neighbor killed," Linden murmured into my chest. His fingers clenched and relaxed against my abs, like a kneading cat settling in for a nap.

I couldn't believe he'd remembered the thread of that conversation. Fucking him drove it right the hell out of my head.

"Not too much to tell. She mom-voiced me, and the next thing I knew I was driving out to see her and check out the neighbor. He was this nutso bastard who thought he could blow the shitty air out of his house on smoggy days by using a leafblower. All the time. Inside his house."

"A leafblower? A...thing that blows leaves?"

Right, not a lot of yard work going on in a coffee shop, and he didn't have a frame of reference for anything else in the human world. "Basically. Like a giant vacuum cleaner, only it blows the air out instead of pulling it in. And it's really fucking loud. This asshole ran it with all his doors and windows open at midnight, and three in the morning, and five in the morning, and then all day. This poor woman was losing her shit because she and her kids hadn't slept decently in weeks. So...yeah, I mean, it sucks to say I enjoyed killing him. But I really, really did. What a dick."

Linden shook against me, the vibrations and his nearness almost getting my cock perked up again. It took a second to figure out he was laughing.

"It was a public service? Is that what you're going with?"

"You should've heard it, okay?" I knew I sounded a little defensive, but—okay, yeah, I was a little defensive. People didn't usually laugh at my job. "So fucking loud. I ended up trying to turn down her money, but she insisted. Said she wanted to have the satisfaction of killing him second-hand. And then she strolled back into the house to bake cookies with her kids. Swear to God, if she wasn't married and I wasn't, you know, me, I might've asked her to have dinner with me."

Linden stopped laughing, and he went a little stiff. "I guess women are more your preference, then?"

Like most guys, I could be kind of slow on the uptake sometimes, but that was obvious enough even for me. I twisted my neck and pressed a kiss into his hair, giving him a squeeze. "Gorgeous and stubborn are my preference."

"Oh." Linden nuzzled into my chest, back to acting like a sleepy cat again. I wished I had him naked under a pile of blankets, with all the time in the world to be kneaded and pressed and snuggled into exactly the position he liked the best. Taking charge during sex worked for me. I didn't mind being accommodating afterwards. But there wasn't much accommodation to be found on the lumpy dirt. "Okay."

His breathing evened out quickly after that, and I took five minutes, no more and no less, to enjoy it.

After that, I went to sleep too. I'd wake at dawn, and this wouldn't be real anymore.

Chapter Fourteen

Linden

Riding to my death wasn't much more comfortable than walking to it, it turned out.

I shifted in the saddle for the hundredth time. It might have been more comfortable if I hadn't been so completely, gloriously fucked the night before. But I couldn't complain. Every twinge reminded me that I'd had one night of happiness before what was to come.

And it grew closer with every passing moment. We'd left the forest an hour or so before, passing into the grassy rolling hills and valleys nearer to Lady Lisandra's villa. Silver-glinting streams wound through green-velvet slopes peppered with wildflowers in every imaginable color, with the midday sun pouring down and transforming it all into a stained-glass masterpiece.

My mother might be suffering terribly. At the least, fear for me and for herself would be a torture on its own.

And yet the world shone so brightly.

"Another two hours from here," Oskar said. He rode a little ahead of me, and he hadn't spoken to me much that morning. Or looked at me. He'd frowned at Callum and then ignored him too.

I probably hadn't been quiet enough the night before.

Luckily, Oskar couldn't see me blushing, since he refused to acknowledge me.

Callum and Kaspar were riding double to my right, and I glanced at them out of the corner of my eye. It made the most sense to put Callum with Kaspar, since Callum couldn't ride at all and Kaspar was a far better horseman than I was.

Still. Seeing Callum's hands on Kaspar's waist set my teeth on edge. Kaspar was gorgeous and stubborn, probably far more than I could claim. And his long hair kept blowing back in Callum's face.

Callum had slid out from under me at the first hint of dawn, leaving his jacket over me but picking up his gun and walking away without a word. He'd returned a few minutes later, probably after taking a piss and stretching out his sore muscles, but he could've woken me with a kiss, couldn't he? Or kissed me when he returned?

He did neither, and when I handed his jacket back, he took it with a grunt of thanks and a few words about getting on the road. No tenderness. Nothing at all to mark the way we'd slept so closely, after being so intimately joined.

Callum couldn't even kiss me, and I'd be sore from his hard possession of me for—probably the rest of my life.

I couldn't muster so much as a smile. Oskar probably would've laughed, though. That was more his sense of humor than mine.

No one said another word for the next hour and a half.

Oskar reined in his horse as we reached the bottom of a small, sheltered valley between three hills. I knew every inch of this ground; I'd tumbled and ridden and run up and down every slope, picnicked under the spreading oak at one end of it, caught and released bright green and blue frogs in the pond at the other. We were nearly home, and this was the end.

"We need a plan," Oskar said.

"Hard to make one of those without any intel," Callum

answered him. "Can we get down—dismount, whatever, while we talk about it? Fuck this."

I couldn't have agreed more. I'd rather have been riding Callum. At least that, even if it hurt nearly as much in my current well-used state, might've been worth the pain.

We led the horses to the pond to water them, and Oskar and Kaspar started to argue. Oskar wanted to leave Kaspar and me behind, with Kaspar using as much magic as he could to conceal us, while he and Callum mounted a full-on assault. They'd taken twelve of Lord Evalt's men the night before, Oskar pointed out. And although Evalt possessed powerful sorcery, he didn't have a huge army. He might only have the same number or a few more at the villa. And rumors had it that Evalt commanded his men through magical compulsion. We might not even need to kill all of them—killing Evalt could be enough to end it then and there.

"It would be better to circle around the villa and come in through the gardens," Kaspar contended. "He might already know we're here. We may have bought some time, eliminating his men in the ambush, and I cast what spells I could this morning to hide us from his crows. But the closer we get to him, the stronger his magic will be. If one of his crows flies overhead now, it'll see us. Besides which, he knows we're coming. We don't have a choice in that, given his threats. No one who doesn't live there knows about the gate at the bottom of the orchard. It's hidden behind vines. We may be able to get in that way, and it's certainly better than marching up to the front door!"

"If you'd rather skulk like a coward—"

"You've been telling me to skulk like a coward from the beginning, while you take all the glory!" Kaspar retorted. "Besides, we don't know where Evalt's keeping the hostages! How is it skulking or cowardly to take what little advantage we have, to try to see what we're facing before we're in the thick of it?"

Oskar began to argue vociferously, again, in favor of his own plan, and I stared down at the pond, at the ripples fanning out from my mount's muzzle as she drank her fill and the way they made the leaves of the water lilies bob and dance. Callum's frowning reflection caught my eye. Why didn't he speak? He had to have an opinion. It wasn't like him to hold it back.

But he stayed tight-lipped, his brow furrowed.

If he didn't intend to offer anything, I had to. I'd had enough. We were wasting time. My mother would die within hours, and nearly everyone I knew and loved with her.

"Kaspar's right," I said—loudly. "We need to do something soon, and his plan is the best anyone has suggested. Unless there are better ideas?" I turned to Callum, hoping he'd take that as an opening, but he didn't. He didn't even look back at me.

"You've made your point," Oskar growled. "The garden gate. But this isn't how honorable men wage war. And you and Linden ought to stay behind."

"Not a chance, and this is how men who want to live wage war," Kaspar snapped. "Besides, we're not at war and honorable men don't take ladies hostage and don't deserve the courtesies of a formal conflict."

"We ought to go," I said, feeling as if I'd been teetering on the brink of a cliff and had taken a step into free fall as I did. There was nothing else to say, nothing left to do but face the man who'd wanted me dead since he learned about my birth. "We need to go."

Oskar, Kaspar and I mounted our horses again, but Callum shook his head as Kaspar offered him a hand up. "I'll walk from here," he said. "I've had enough horseback riding to last me a lifetime." His words hung in the air, the implication that it might be a short one as clear as if he'd said it. "Anyway, I'll take rear guard."

"Suit yourself," Kaspar said, and we were off.

Oskar rode ahead, with Kaspar and me abreast behind him, and Callum dropped back. When I twisted my neck to catch a glimpse of him, I found him pacing along about five yards behind, his gun out and his face blank.

The hills drew together at the northern end of the valley, creating a narrow passage leading to a rocky field where Lady Lisandra's herdsmen often kept a flock of sheep. We rode through it in single file, Oskar, and then Kaspar, and then me, with Callum trailing behind. Our horses' hooves thudded softly on the deep grass, and otherwise I heard nothing. It was as if we were alone in the whole world.

As Kaspar passed through the gap, I glimpsed the field spread out before us, empty of anything but scattered boulders and waving grass.

And the moment I passed through behind him, the air wavered as if we were seeing a mirage, and too many black-armored soldiers to count materialized, their bows and swords out and pointed at us. Oskar roared in rage and drew his sword, but they'd already surrounded him, the soldiers pulling him from the saddle and overwhelming him. My heart pounded and my chest felt like it'd frozen up, no breaths coming in or out—ancestors, this was it, they were going to kill me here, and I'd never see my mother again, never drink wine, or make love—and then Kaspar and I were on the ground, and my arms were pulled roughly behind my back.

The soldiers' shouts of triumph echoed harshly in my ringing ears. But they didn't kill me. Instead, they marched me away, all but dragging me across the field. I couldn't see Kaspar or Oskar and—where was Callum? I twisted my head, trying to find him, but the men crowding around me filled my vision. One of them shoved me between the shoulder blades so roughly I nearly fell, crying out in pain as my arms twisted, my wrists held cruelly by the man behind me.

I kept waiting for the sharp reports of Callum's gun, for the men carrying me away to fall one by one.

They didn't come.

Callum didn't come. He'd abandoned us.

Callum

The second Oskar and Kaspar started arguing about the best way to take Evalt and his men by surprise, I knew we were fucked. Evalt knew we were coming, because he'd sent us an invitation we couldn't refuse; he knew where we were coming from, because his crows had seen us there; he knew when we'd arrive, because he'd set the timeframe. His ambush hadn't worked, and maybe he'd been thrown off a little by that, but it wasn't much to count on. When his men didn't come back, with or without us, he'd assume we were still on the way.

So hidden garden gate or no hidden garden gate, I doubted we'd surprise anyone. I'd been hoping Oskar and Kaspar had some real trick up their sleeves, but it didn't sound like it. At all. Realistically, we were going to be captured, and quickly.

Or...*they* were, if I stayed back and gave myself the opportunity to slip away before I was noticed, while Evalt's men focused on the other three. I'd been mulling it over all morning. Evalt might not know about me. I was the surprise, I was the trick.

And I had to figure out how to make that work for us on my own. Telling Oskar, who I'd already seen liked to operate as bluntly and openly as possible, that I meant to 'skulk like a coward' while he, Kaspar, and Linden walked into an obvious trap? Not something that would've flown. Oskar wouldn't have listened, and we didn't have time to fight over it.

So I took rear guard, stayed off the horses, and hung back, far enough that I could make my own decisions without a goddamn committee.

And it was a good fucking thing, too. The second Oskar, Kaspar, and Linden rode out of the little valley we'd stopped in, and into the open, a whole army came out of fucking nowhere, like someone had pulled back a curtain. God, I'd never get used to magic. Oskar went down immediately, because these soldiers had the common sense to neutralize the biggest threat first. Kaspar and

Linden didn't stand a chance, and they were pulled off their horses and bound within seconds.

That made up my mind for me. If it'd looked like the soldiers meant to execute them right then and there, I'd have intervened. There wouldn't have been another choice. But dragging them off to Evalt seemed to be the plan, and that meant I still had time to come up with something better than going down shooting.

I'd scoped out the hills on either side of the valley's mouth as we approached, and as soon as the soldiers appeared I scrambled up the hill to my left. A couple of trees and a rock sat at the crown of the hill—cover.

I ducked behind the rock and poked my head up enough to get a look at the situation below. Fourteen men, now that I had a vantage point to count them, with Oskar hogtied and still struggling and being dragged along by six of them, with the other eight surrounding Linden and Kaspar.

As I watched, Linden tried to look over his shoulder. I caught a glimpse of his pale, terrified face before one of the bastards thumped him with his fist and shoved him forward again.

Fuck. He'd been looking for me. He probably thought I'd up and run, giving it up for a bad job.

Not much I could do about that. If he died, or I died, before we saw each other again…it made me sick, that he might never know I hadn't ditched him and left him to die.

But there wasn't any choice. Hand-to-hand like that, they'd have taken me down as fast as Oskar. I might've gotten a couple of shots off first, but then it would've been over. Now, if I'd had my rifle, and they hadn't had hostages…it felt good for a millisecond, imagining how I'd have picked them off one by one, head shot after head shot.

But I had a single fifteen-round magazine for my Sig, no intel, and no backup. Very fucking John McClane. At least I had shoes.

As soon as the whole troop had gotten out of hearing range, I scrambled back down the hill and set off parallel and to the left.

I trailed them across a large rocky field, and then hung back as they turned onto a small path leading further to my right. Probably to the front door, and if I was wrong about that, then I was extra fucked.

I circled around, double-timing it in what I could hope might be the direction of the back of the house.

I had a hidden garden gate to find—and then hopefully a plan, and some snappy one-liners, would come to me when I needed them. And I could only pray that Lord Evalt was the monologuing type of asshole villain. The least he could do would be to buy me some time.

Chapter Fifteen

Linden

More soldiers stood on guard at the villa's wrought-pewter gates, one of which hung crookedly on its hinges, the spread-winged phoenix at the top of it bent and dangling. Lady Lisandra's violets, which had grown in profusion in beds along the gravel drive to the front door, lay in trampled smears. My cheeks were wet, though I hadn't realized I'd been crying.

A shout of triumph went up as our captors wrestled us through the gates. My feet skidded in the gravel, and ahead of me, Oskar struggled anew, managing to kick one of the soldiers holding him in the knee with a horrid crunch. Another soldier cuffed Oskar upside the head, and they pulled him onward.

The villa rose before me, white stone and climbing roses and broad windows glittering in the sun. Home. The place where I'd been born, the place where I would die.

It felt inevitable now. I could only pray Lord Evalt would spare my mother, though I knew Oskar and Kaspar would die with me. No, he'd kill everyone. Lady Lisandra didn't have much influence, as fae aristocracy went, but if she survived she'd carry her grievances to the High Court. Evalt had, so far, managed to avoid any conflicts with those more powerful than he, and if he killed all the witnesses and spun a web of half-truths to account for his actions, no one would bother to avenge us. It was the way of our people, to shrug and ignore anything that didn't overstep our own territorial boundaries. But if Lady Lisandra lived to bring a formal petition, marked in her noble blood, the Queen would be forced to take notice.

He would kill us all. He had no choice, now that he'd set himself on this path. My only hope had been that we might somehow sneak in and take Evalt by surprise. My stomach clenched, heavy and sick, as the full realization of how stupid I'd been sank in.

He had too many men. We were never going to succeed. And Oskar, more experienced in matters like this, must have guessed that would be the case, no matter how bravely he'd tried to fight it out to the bitter end. If he knew it, so did Kaspar. They'd willingly walked into this for my sake, so that I wouldn't need to face it alone.

Callum had more sense than any of us.

If only the seer had been right, and I really was destined to kill Evalt…but that couldn't be true. I knew it in my bones.

No matter how I dragged my feet, it took only moments to be pulled up the broad steps and through the front door, and into the spacious hall. The soldiers shoved Oskar and Kaspar to their knees, prying their jaws open and forcing leather straps between their teeth to keep them silent.

Two of the men flung open the huge, ornately carved double doors to Lady Lisandra's ballroom, and the rest manhandled us all inside. They pulled Oskar and Kaspar to the side of the room, allowing me to see what lay before me.

Deep, ugly gouges marred the parquet floor of the ballroom. More soldiers lined the walls.

And in a great wooden throne-like chair at the far end sat Lord Evalt, clad in black robes trimmed with gold, and with his black hair and beard flowing over his chest and shoulders like ink. His shrunken, white-eyed seer sat beside him on an ottoman. Lady

Lisandra and my mother, holding hands, knelt before him. Lady Lisandra's cheek bloomed red and purple with a swollen bruise, and her hip-length mahogany curls hung loose and tangled around her torso. Blood stained her torn silver robes.

My mother looked less battered, possibly because she hadn't fought as vigorously; Lady Lisandra was quite the swordswoman, and I doubted they'd taken her without losing a man or two in the process. But I took after my mother, and neither of us had any skill with implements of war. Her plain gray dress didn't have any blood on it, thank the ancestors, but her hair, pale blonde like mine, was frizzy and mussed, and her face was bone-white except for her red and puffy eyes.

When she saw me, her mouth fell open, a hand flying up to her face. New tears spilled over, trickling down her beautiful face and glinting like diamonds. I didn't know what to wish for, that she died first and didn't need to watch Evalt slit my throat, or that he killed me first, so that my last moments wouldn't be an agony of grief.

As if it mattered much at all.

My mother's mouth moved, but no sound came out.

And Lord Evalt laughed. It rolled around the room like a peal of thunder, rich and deep and far too resonant for the lungs of a normal man. "Your whore of a mother made too much noise, and I tired of her whining," he said, his voice less full than his laugh but still enough to reach every corner of the ballroom. "I silenced her. Don't fret. I'll give back her voice in time for you to hear her final scream."

Well. That answered the question of whom he intended to kill first.

"This isn't necessary," I said, my voice quavering, even more pathetic in contrast to Evalt's arrogance. Oh, couldn't I at least *sound* brave? "I never wanted to kill you. I was never meant to kill you. Your seer has it wrong."

"So you would like me to believe." Evalt languidly raised one long, ring-bedecked hand and brought it down across my mother's cheek. Her head snapped back, and I knew she cried out, though she made no sound. Lady Lisandra caught her, cradling her against her shoulder, and if she could've killed Evalt with a look alone, he'd have dropped dead.

I lunged, howling in horror and rage, and my captors brought me up short, casting me down onto the floor. My cheekbone hit the boards hard, the impact stunning.

"Put them together. We can allow them this last moment, can we not?" Evalt's voice echoed oddly inside my skull along with the ringing in my ears. Footsteps vibrated through the floor, and then my mother and Lady Lisandra landed hard beside me.

My mother caught me in her arms, lifting my torso off the floor and smothering me against her chest. For a moment, one single, shining moment, I closed my eyes, forgot everything else, and breathed her in: the familiar scents of lavender from the sachet she kept in her wardrobe, spices from the kitchen, warmth and safety and love. She shook with silent sobs, her voice still muted. I felt a hand on my shoulder. Lady Lisandra. She squeezed me, and while it could have been comfort, I felt her other message. I needed to sit up, to face Lord Evalt with more courage than this. More dignity than huddling in my mother's lap like a child.

So I struggled up, my mother and Lady Lisandra helping me on either side, and I looked Lord Evalt in the face. "I will not die in fear of you," I said. My voice still shook, but I meant it. I had to mean it, because on either side of me, the two women who had raised me knelt with their backs unbowed. I owed it to them to die with the same strength they possessed.

A slow, sickening smile crept across Evalt's narrow, angular face, his mouth a slash of white in his dark beard. He rose, looming until I had to crane my neck to stare him down, and began to rotate his arms and move his fingers in a complicated flickering dance of magic. Purple sparks shot from his hands in patterns I couldn't interpret, mesmerizing me with awe and horror. "Yes, you will," he said, that smile widening into a rictus grin. "You'll die terrified, and I'll feast on it. On all of you. Every moment of your terror only feeds my magic and makes me stronger."

I leaned closer to my mother, wishing I could put my arms around her as she had hers tightly around my waist. My whole body throbbed with bruises, some from the soldiers' rough handling and some souvenirs of Callum's possession of me the night before. It felt like a lifetime ago. I'd never see him again, and anger warred with relief in my tight, aching chest. Maybe he'd left us to die, but at least he might live. He'd never wanted to be involved in this. He deserved to live, after saving my life in the human realm and fighting side by side with Oskar in the ambush.

It didn't matter that he'd left me. It didn't matter. I'd be glad he lived, that was all.

Lord Evalt took a step forward, and the sparks flowing from him doubled in size, their brightness flaring. "Don't worry," he said. "I'll go slowly enough to savor it."

Callum

Finding the hidden garden gate proved impossible once I'd looped around to the other side of the house, but I didn't try all that hard. I needed speed, not cleverness.

Oskar might've struggled to scale the high wall; he was too heavy. Linden and Kaspar probably didn't have the upper body strength for it. Well, lucky they weren't there. I was trying so fucking hard not to think about why they weren't there, but images of Linden lying dead in front of his mother kept popping into my head, and I had to fight to keep them out.

Focusing on climbing the garden wall helped for a minute, finding footholds in the stone and avoiding the wicked thorns on the vines that grew all over it, and mostly failing at the latter. Stinging gouges covered my palms and fingers by the time I dropped down on the other side, an easy ten-foot fall. Fuck this place. Even the fucking plants were trying to kill me.

The garden might've been a good distraction, too, if I'd had time to stop and gawk at it. I'd never seen plants like that. They looked like something out of an episode of original *Star Trek*, one of the ones where the flowers shot pollen in people's faces and they all started fucking like rabbits. Technicolor and bizarre, with oblong, fleshy shapes that didn't seem like they belonged on my planet. Mixed in were normal things, roses and ferns and crap like that, but that couldn't overcome the overall weirdness.

I cautiously pushed my way through a bush covered in some kind of blue, star-shaped berries, hoping they wouldn't try to eat me, and peeked out through the foliage. I'd managed to get twenty yards from the house, more or less, with the main bulk of the building directly in front of me. It looked like a goddamn wedding cake, all white and fancy and swirly where it didn't need to be. A terrace ran the length of the back of the house, with doors all along it and steps leading down to the garden at intervals. A swath of grass separated the terrace and the flower beds.

Lots of access points.

Too many access points, and too much visibility.

And I could practically hear the clock ticking.

I couldn't see anyone, though, and I couldn't decide if that was a good sign or a bad one. Maybe they weren't expecting any-one to come in through the back of the house. Or maybe there were soldiers fucking everywhere, invisible just like the ones that came out of nowhere in the field.

Two choices: One, creep along the taller bushes at the back of the garden and stay out of sight as long as possible, approaching the house at the end of the terrace, where at least I'd only be visible from a couple of the glass doors, and not fucking all of them at once.

Option two: Run like hell across the garden, and the lawn, and the terrace, and get inside, single gun blazing if necessary.

Linden would probably die either way.

Fuck it. Wasn't like they had snipers on the roof.

I crossed as quickly as I could, staying low and hoping the terrace's stone railings would hide me a little bit. They probably didn't, but it didn't seem to matter; I made it to the terrace without any kind of alarm going up, and I flattened myself against the side of the house between two of the glass doors. I counted to ten. No shouts, no running feet, nothing.

Carefully, I strafed to the left and peered through the door. Not much to see, because the room was so dim, but I didn't catch any movement. This door, or go along the building looking for Linden, or for anything out of the ordinary?

As I glanced down the length of the terrace, I saw something that definitely qualified as out of the ordinary—for me, anyway. A handful of bright purple sparks whizzed out of a window at the end, twirling in a complicated dance and then hanging in the air like fucked-up fireflies.

Yep. That was weird, all right. I'd never claim to be an expert, but evil-looking purple sparks in the air seemed like something an evil sorcerer might be the source of.

I jogged down the terrace, keeping my feet light and almost silent, passing a dozen more window-doors as I went. I glanced in as I passed, but I only saw silent, empty rooms.

Where were all the people who must live here, servants and guards and gardeners? God, I hoped they weren't all dead already. I'd seen the crumpled, broken, stinking aftermaths of massacres. I never wanted to see another.

At the end of the terrace, I found a set of glass doors wider and more ornate than the others, clearly meant to fold all the way back on each side and essentially open a large room to the outdoors. More sparks came out of the glass as I approached, passing through it like they would through empty air.

Magic. My fingers tingled and the hair on the back of my neck rose. Had I gotten more sensitive to this bullshit? I doubted it. Sensitive wasn't exactly my middle name. Probably just my usual bullshit meter, pushed into overdrive by the whole 'about to try to kill an evil sorcerer' thing.

I crouched against the wall, putting my head well below eye level, and risked a look inside.

Yeah, evil sorcerer, all right, complete with flowing robes and purple magic electricity shit sparking out of his fingertips. The asshole had to be nearly seven feet tall, even though he was as thin as a rail. My vantage point gave me the back of his head and a sliver of his profile.

It also gave me a full, unobstructed view of a huge room with a two-story ceiling, the soldiers ranged around the sides, and— Linden. Linden, with his eyes huge in his pale face, bruises and traces of blood discoloring his skin, and his hands tied behind his back. He knelt in front of Evalt between two women I guessed were his mother and Lady Lisandra, the owner of this place.

My heart gave an unsteady lurch. *Just another job*, I reminded myself. *Evalt's another asshole who needs to be put down, and Linden's just another hostage. Collateral damage happens.* Right. Next I'd try to sell myself the Brooklyn Bridge.

Quick count: nine soldiers that I could see, and probably a similar number out of sight along the perimeter of the room I couldn't see. Maybe more somewhere else, but they weren't relevant at the moment.

Even though I'd stayed the hell out of their discussion of strategy and tactics that morning, I'd listened and absorbed every word. Evalt had to go down first. The soldiers might try to intervene, but they were red herrings. If Oskar had it right, they'd stop fighting once Evalt died.

I had a clear path to Evalt, and even better, a clear shot, even though firing through glass of unknown composition and strength wasn't ideal.

I'd need to back up enough not to get creamed by the shattering door, and might be seen as soon as I did. Deep breath. I had one try at this.

I jumped up, took four quick steps back, and aimed for the

center of Evalt's torso, keeping the barrel as perpendicular to the glass as possible.

And I fired, once, twice, a quick double tap. The deafening crash and tinkle of shattering glass drowned out the pop-pop of the shots. I fired once more for good measure, even though the reflections off the glass shards falling and spinning gave me no visibility at all. But my aim was good. I hadn't wavered from my original target.

And then the glass clashed to the ground and settled. Evalt had turned to face me, but—the motherfucker had turned to face me. Not a scratch on him, not a drop of blood, not a rip in those stupid fucking pretentious robes. He bared his teeth, his eyes like dark whirlpools. I'd seen saner eyes on fuckers deemed too crazy to stand trial for murder.

My bullets hadn't touched him.

I fired again, twice more, dead center into his chest. Or rather, right up to his chest. The bullets just—stopped, right there in mid-air, and fell to the floor with a sad little patter and clunk.

"A human," Evalt said, his voice too big to have come out of a narrow chest like that. Round and rolling. He could've fronted a Tennessee Ernie Ford cover band. "How interesting. Your weapons can't injure me, you insignificant insect. I'll disassemble his physical form first," Evalt threw over his shoulder at Linden. "So you can see how you'll die."

He raised his hands, and they started to glow, shooting out more and more sparks and humming like a high-voltage line. Behind him, Linden stared at me, his lips parted. The lower one had been split by someone's rough hand. I thought I saw him mouth my name.

And that was fucking enough. Some men might've taken offense to 'insignificant insect,' but I'd been called worse, even if you didn't count 'mundane tool.' Some men might've emptied the rest of the magazine into Evalt's chest on a desperate hope, or maybe run.

I'd have been smart to run.

I wasn't offended, and I obviously wasn't all that smart, either. But I *was* fucking irritated, out of patience with bullshit, and not in the mood to be physically disassembled, or whatever the fuck.

Evalt's men had started to close in, shifting away from the walls and moving toward their master. I eyed them warily. They seemed to be hanging back, waiting for Evalt to handle me himself, but ready to rush me if it seemed to be going my way.

I could use my last few shots on them...but no. Evalt remained the primary target, even though I remembered now what Oskar had said about weapons forged under the sun.

I shoved the Sig back in its holster. Fine. So no weapon could kill this son of a bitch. So fucking what. I'd killed a dude with a paperclip once, for fuck's sake.

When I stuck my hand in my pocket, no paperclips appeared—but I found the flashlight. Not a weapon. But just as deadly as a weapon, if you were me...and plastic wasn't forged.

Evalt flung his arms wide, clearly preparing for a magical crescendo. His men froze, hands on their weapons but obviously trusting in Evalt's magic to take down the human intruder.

I sprinted at him. Evalt's men shouted and burst into motion at last, but before they could get to me I pulled the flashlight out of my pocket and thwacked the butt end of it directly through Evalt's right eye socket with the heel of my hand. The meaty, sickening squelch and crunch echoed through the room, even over the soldiers' footsteps and belated cries of alarm.

Evalt swayed, his arms slowly windmilling and then dropping to his sides, and then he listed and started to topple, his remaining eye rolling back in his head. A little, shrunken woman who'd been on a footstool nearby leapt to her feet, flinging her arms around Evalt and letting out an earsplitting shriek.

And the magic that'd been building up in Evalt's hands detonated like a grenade. The shockwave struck me right across the chest and hit his men as they grabbed for me, knocking us all back like bowling pins. The seer's scream cut off as she melted into a spray of purple light and body parts, and Evalt went up in a spout of sparks, his robes disintegrating and his face, and my flashlight, warping and sliding down his body like they'd been—disassembled.

I collapsed to my knees, my hair standing on end, my extremities burning, and everything in between hot and bright and too tight and too hot—

I slid to the ground, gasping, my lungs solid lumps of fire. No air in. No air out. No fucking air.

If I'd predicted the top ten ways I'd expected to die, getting my physical form disassembled by a purple-sparking sorcerer in robes wouldn't have made the list.

Linden. Linden had been right behind Evalt. Far enough to be outside the blast radius? It'd been aimed at me, not him. Maybe a shorter radius, in Linden's direction.

That would be good enough. Saving Linden would be good enough. Wasn't there some book I'd skimmed in high school, a better thing I do today, or something? I'd fucking hated that book.

Air. I needed it, but couldn't get it. Couldn't feel my hands anymore, or my face. The floor vibrated under me. More screams.

Fuck, I hoped Jesse had survived somehow. I'd never know. But Linden—

And that was all she wrote.

Chapter Sixteen

Callum

"I think he's waking up!" Linden's voice?

"He absorbed too much magic, Linden. I think that's his nervous system overloading. I'm so sorry. I have no idea how to counter it. I don't know if he'll survive." Probably Kaspar, there.

Me? Were they talking about me? I blinked, catching a quick glimpse of a circle of faces leaning over me, sort of like the viewpoint a zoo animal might have if it also got stuck at the bottom of a well.

Another blink. Linden knelt beside me, and I'd started to get back enough feeling to know he had my hand in a death grip. I'd be able to tell the touch of his skin from anyone's. Warmth spread up my arm, and it had nothing to do with his fingers themselves, which felt ice-cold. I tried to squeeze them.

The floor didn't feel as hard as I expected. Right, not a floor. I lay on some kind of sofa, probably one of the pieces of furniture that had been along the walls of the room. Nice of them to move me.

One more blink, and this time I managed to keep my eyes open. Right beside Linden, with her hand on his shoulder, stood his mother, her blonde hair an exact match for her son's and her blue eyes nearly as beautiful. Kaspar hovered near my feet, with Oskar standing right next to him and glowering down at me. The woman I assumed to be Lady Lisandra stood on the other side of me from Linden. She'd been all bedraggled when she'd been Evalt's captive, yet somehow she'd already managed to get her long hair piled up on her head in some sort of complicated bun, and the rest of her looked pristine. Magic. Jesus.

No threats in the immediate vicinity.

I flicked my eyes back to Linden. He had tear-tracks down his cheeks, the whites of his eyes were mostly red at this point, and his eyelids had swollen to twice their normal size. The bruises still marred his skin.

I'd never seen anything so beautiful.

And then he smiled.

I wasn't a poetic kind of man. I'd hardly ever read an entire poem, even in school, except a couple by Emily Dickinson. They were like ten lines, short lines at that, and I could handle that much.

They hadn't prepared me to try to describe Linden's smile, not even a little bit. The sun came out, the room faded away, and his eyes glowed like stars.

I could see why Evalt thought Linden fit some kind of prophecy about the bringer of light.

And then it hit me, as blinding as Evalt's ridiculous purple magic sparks, and I started to laugh. Score one for petty theft. I'd brought a light, all right. A cheap flashlight with no batteries, with a circumference that fit perfectly in a homicidal maniac's eye socket.

"Is he having a seizure?" Oskar demanded. "Is he going to die after all?"

"Fuck off, Oskar," I rasped out, my throat feeling like I'd swallowed a bucket of sand. "No such luck." Lady Lisandra frowned down at me. Shit. I had the manners of a—well, a soldier-turned-hitman with no female relatives. "Sorry, uh, ma'am.

Ma'ams." Linden's mother. Fuck. Way to meet the parent.

"Callum," Linden said softly. "I thought you were dying. You've been unconscious for half an hour."

Took more than a magic hand grenade to kill me, apparently. I could feel my whole body now, and it wasn't too bad, actually. A little like that one time I'd been dosed with ecstasy in a club, only not as fun. Similar tingles, but not in the same pleasant places.

"Nah." I shoved myself up onto my other elbow, since I wasn't letting go of Linden's hand for anything. He looked down at the floor, his cheeks flushing. Fuck. What was I supposed to say to him, in front of all these people? I wasn't even sure what I *wanted* to say. I knew what I wanted to do: carry him off somewhere and bury my face in his hair and breathe him in like some kind of freak. Feel his slim body all wrapped up in my arms. Taste him. Not the time, not the place, and I couldn't seem to find a middle ground between all of that and 'Nah.' I looked up at Oskar. "Help me up, big guy?"

Between Oskar's tugging and Linden's petting, I got to my feet. The giant room stood empty except for the six of us. Empty of anyone alive, at least. Evalt and the weird woman who'd screamed like a banshee still lay on the ground. Shreds of them, anyway. But all the soldiers had gone.

"Where is everyone? Lady—Lisandra, right?" She nodded. "Evalt's soldiers. And your people, your household. What happened?"

"The compulsion broke when you killed Evalt, Lord Callum," Lady Lisandra said. Wait, lord *what*? What the fuck? "Some of their minds broke with it. They have been removed while we separate the wheat from the chaff. Some were guilty men before Evalt changed them. Others were not." She shrugged. "My household is well, thanks to you. They were prisoners, but have now been freed."

"I'm glad to hear it. I'm not a lord, by the way. Just Callum."

"You bested Evalt in single combat, Lord Callum," Lady

Lisandra said with way, way too much fucking casualness. "His lands and title are yours by right. May you enjoy them in good health." Lands and title? Oh, what the fuck, for real. "For now, you are my honored guest, and you honor me by accepting my humble hospitality. Linden, perhaps you will show Lord Callum to the blue suite and see to it that he is given all attentions. Lord Callum, I will speak with you later this evening, as I'm sure you have many questions, as do I. Boys, you may supervise the cleaning of this mess on my floor before you see to Evalt's men. Silvi, will you assist me with the wounded?"

Linden's mother—Silvi, apparently—shot me a very, very suspicious look, the kind that promised future bodily harm if necessary, glanced pointedly at where I still held Linden's hand, and then kissed Linden's cheek and followed Lady Lisandra as she swept away out of the room.

I stared after Lady Lisandra. She and that woman who'd hired me to kill her neighbor needed to have coffee together sometime. Or maybe not. They'd probably plot world domination by the second donut.

A glance at Oskar and Kaspar showed me matching sullen frowns. "Boys?"

Kaspar grimaced. "She's our cousin. Older cousin."

"On two different sides of the family," Oskar put in with what seemed like a little too much emphasis. "She is my cousin, and she is Kaspar's cousin. We are not cousins."

Well, wasn't that interesting. At another time I'd have kept pushing, just for the pleasure of watching Oskar squirm. But I had other fish to fry, like getting Linden alone as soon as humanly—or maybe not-humanly—possible. His silence had started to worry me. Did he still think I'd taken off without giving a fuck about him? Did he think I'd had a change of heart along the way, or remembered Evalt had to die to ensure my own safety too? If Evalt had lived, even if I'd escaped I'd have been stranded here, with no allies and nowhere to go. Did he think I'd been selfish to hide when he was captured and then selfish again when I came back?

That might not be completely out of character for me, granted. But I hadn't been thinking about anything but him, and it stung that he'd believe the worst of me, even if he had every reason to. Especially if he had every reason to.

He hadn't let go of my hand. That was something.

Right as that passed through my mind, he let go of my hand, shifting away from me at the same time to put a respectable amount of distance between us.

Well, fuck.

"Okay, not-cousins," I said, trying for lightly sarcastic and hitting heavy and grim. "Get to work. You have a floor to clean. Linden, can we…?"

His cheeks red and his eyes downcast, Linden nodded and led the way.

He didn't look at me or speak to me the whole way up to the room I'd been given. A long hall, and then a wide, twisting staircase, and then another long hall lined with portraits of people in bizarre clothing, and the whole way he kept his eyes fixed firmly ahead of us.

At last he opened a door and stepped inside, keeping a hand on the knob and staying well out of my way while I followed. He hovered there, not making any move to close the door behind us. I glanced around. Huge bed, blue wall hangings, lots of things trimmed with gold. Not my usual digs.

"I'll leave you to rest, Lord Callum," Linden said quietly while I stood there gaping at my surroundings.

And then the little fucker tried to make a break for it.

Which was not fucking happening. That or the 'Lord Callum' bullshit. I took his wrist in a firm grip and removed his hand from the door, and then shut the door myself. I twisted the key in the lock for good measure.

Linden finally looked up at me, his lips turned down and his eyes watery. God, fuck this. I'd saved his life and killed his mortal enemy so he wouldn't have to be afraid, or upset, or unhappy. That smile he'd given me when I woke up…it really had been like pure sunshine. I hadn't realized until then how dimmed he'd been ever since I'd known him.

And he'd still sucked me in, still taken my breath away. I knew that if he really did go back to normal, if he shone as brightly as he naturally should, I'd be lost. Utterly fucked.

It didn't matter. I'd deal with that. Linden shouldn't look like this.

"Everyone's alive," I said. "Everyone who should be alive, anyway. Your mom's safe. We all survived. So all I can think is that I've done something wrong. You need to tell me what it is, so I can fix it." Fuck, what if I'd hurt him the night before? What if he'd come out of all the adrenaline and worry and figured out he hadn't really wanted me after all? "If you need me to fuck off, I will."

But my fingers tightened around his wrist as the words left my mouth, and I wasn't so sure I could follow through on that, even if he begged me. My fingers tightened a little more. The fragile bones of his wrist dug into my palm, and his pulse pounded wildly.

"You killed Evalt and fulfilled a dread prophecy," Linden said, the words dragging out of him in a way that sounded painful, his voice hoarse. "And now you're a rich and powerful man, and your renown will spread to every distant corner of the realm. I'm a servant here, Lord Cal—"

Nope. No, no, and triple fucking no.

I wrapped my other arm around his waist, hauled him flush against me, and kissed the living daylights out of him. He struggled a little, even though his lips parted under mine the second I touched him, eager and sweet and soft. Linden tasted a little like tears and a little like the same scent he carried with him, something bright and crisp and fresh. I ignored his wiggling. Well, I didn't quite ignore it, since it rubbed his perfect body against me really, really enjoyably.

But I didn't let him go. I kissed him, and then kissed him some more, nibbling his plump lower lip and licking into his mouth and chasing the taste of him, until he'd bent back over my arm and gone completely, beautifully pliant. The hand I didn't have pinned crept up to my shoulder and held on tight, and he kissed me back.

I moved down to his neck after a while, and I needed more leverage. The enormous bed...but we were both filthy, and I didn't want to rub purple Evalt-residue all over the bed, since I had plans for it later after Linden and I got clean.

I shoved him up against the wall by the door instead and wedged my thigh between his legs, pressing up enough to make him gasp.

"Please don't," Linden moaned, even as he squirmed against my leg. "Please. This isn't—you're not—you're a lord now, and I'm not *anyone*."

Fuck. Did he think I was—taking advantage of him? The magic-realm equivalent of a rich asshole hitting on the maid when his wife wasn't looking?

I pulled back from his neck with an effort. The skin there felt so soft between my lips and between my teeth. I wanted to mark him up everywhere.

Or even worse, even more unbelievable, did he think he should be—what, staying in his place? I stared at him, taking in his tortured expression, caught somewhere between arousal and misery. What the fuck was I supposed to do now?

And then it came to me, as easy as breathing.

"What Lady Lisandra said. About single combat. Does it have to be to the death, or what?"

Linden blinked at me, his lips parted. "What?"

"Does it?" I demanded. "Did I have to kill him, to get all his lordliness and everything?"

"No, you didn't," Linden said slowly, his brow furrowing. I

wanted to kiss those little lines away. Kiss him all over. "If he had formally yielded, that would have been enough. Lord Callum—"

"Stop fucking calling me that," I snapped. "Now hit me."

"Hit you."

"Yeah, hit me, like with your hand—"

The slap came out of nowhere, with a surprisingly genuine amount of force behind it. My cheek stung like a bitch. Linden pulled his hand back, letting out a shocked little sound, like he hadn't expected to want to smack me across the face quite as much as he did.

The impact wasn't much. I'd given myself worse bumping into walls after one too many bourbons. But it zinged straight down, my half-hard cock perking up another notch, and I grinned at him.

Linden cringed back against the wall like he expected me to retaliate. Instead, I leaned in and kissed him softly, just once, letting my lips linger for a second.

"I formally yield," I whispered against his mouth.

Linden went completely rigid. "What do you mean?"

I pulled back again, enough that I could look him in the eyes. And try not to get distracted by how blue they were. I sort of succeeded. "I mean I yield. You hit me, I yielded, single combat achieved. Congratulations, Lord Linden. My lands and title are all fucking yours."

His eyes widened until I thought they might take over his face. "You're insane," he choked out. "You're—that's madness. That's not how it works! You don't mean that!"

I shrugged and ground my leg against his cock a little bit, pressing my own against his abs. That felt so fucking good. He needed to get with the transfer-of-lordliness program, because I had to be inside him or I was going to lose it.

"I mean it, that is how it works because you just told me so, and yeah, maybe I'm crazy, but I'm also not interested in being a lord. So now *you're* a lord, and I'm nothing more than some asshole who killed a sorcerer and really wants to fuck you. No—conflict of interest. Yes or no, Linden?"

"Oh," he gasped. "Oh. But you'd make an excellent lord. You're a soldier. They'd respect you. They wouldn't respect me."

"They'll respect you, or I'll fucking kill all of them," I growled. "Me. Fucking you. Yes or no?" I slid my hand down his back and palmed his ass, pressing my fingers between his cheeks.

"Yes, Callum, yes—"

And that was all I needed to hear.

Chapter Seventeen

Linden

Callum stripped me so quickly I almost couldn't follow his movements, a blur of my clothes flying in all directions, and his mouth catching at my throat and then my chest, little stinging nips interspersed with the flicker of his tongue, soothing the marks he'd made.

And then he was on his knees, biting at my inner thighs, his hands pressing my legs apart until I had to brace myself against the wall with both hands. His hair wasn't long enough to hold onto anyway, and I had no idea how he'd react if I tried.

My head spun, the room whirling around me dizzily. I closed my eyes as he sucked a mark into my hip, murmuring something that sounded too complimentary to be true, something about how beautiful I was, how much he wanted me, his voice low and hoarse. He couldn't really think I was worth giving up a title, a fortune, a place of honor, could he? He hadn't meant it. He'd take me again, his blood up from the fight, and then he'd forget me.

*They'll respect you, or I'll fucking kill all of them...*he couldn't have meant that. Hoping otherwise felt masochistic, when that hope had to be dashed eventually. He'd need to stay for that. He'd need to want to stay with me forever for that...

My cock stood out straight and hard and ready, aching for his touch. It didn't seem to care about any of that. "Please, Callum," I said, sounding like a desperate whore. I didn't care either, it seemed. "Please, take me in your mouth, and then fuck me, put me on the floor and fuck me…"

The words lost all meaning, trailing away into a moan as he swallowed me down. Callum sucked cock like he did everything else, with dangerous focus and more intensity than I could bear. It didn't take long. I writhed against the wall, cried out, and came in his hand as he pulled his mouth off and stroked me through my spasms.

Exhaustion hit me hard as the pleasure receded. All my limbs went limp at once.

I thought I heard Callum mutter, "A place this nice has to have a bathroom somewhere," and then he was moving me, pulling me away from the wall and manhandling me—somewhere. I kept my eyes closed and let myself slump against his broad chest. He felt so warm and so safe. Maybe he'd hold me again while I slept. Lady Lisandra had meant to talk to him, later, and he'd be asking her to send him home, I was sure of it. I could seize a few hours of forgetfulness in his arms first, though. I hoped.

Instead, the shock of a wet cloth on my cheek snapped me out of it, and I hissed in surprise as my eyes popped open. Callum had set me down on a chair in the suite's bath chamber, leaned me back, and crouched down beside me. He'd found the sink and the towels, too.

"What are you doing?" I managed to ask, barely coherently enough to count as speech.

"Cleaning you up a little," Callum said. "Then cleaning myself up a little. That bed's too nice to get in all filthy. Then," he went on as I opened my mouth again, "I'm going to grab one of those bottles of bath oil over there and fuck you unconscious."

My mouth quirked, the closest I could come to a smile. "Not much of a challenge right now, I don't think. You could—find

148

better uses for your time. I could use my mouth for you, too. Easier."

Callum stopped dabbing at my face and sank back on his heels, glaring at me, his dark eyes intent. "If I wanted easy, I wouldn't be trying to seduce a lord of fairyland, of all the fucking things. And if you can actually think of a better use of my time than fucking the most perfect ass in two realms, then I'm all ears."

If I hadn't been so completely worn out, my next words would never have escaped. "You really think my ass is perfect?"

Callum looked away from me in favor of staring down at the cloth in his hand. "I think you're perfect," he muttered. His cheekbones flushed dull red.

"I'm not a lord," I said. "I'm a cook's son, I can't fight, I can't do anything—"

His gaze flicked back up, and now he looked furious. "Who the fuck told you any of that mattered? You can smile, and the sun comes out. Fuck," he said, breaking off, breathing hard. "Linden, do you want me? Or was last night just a reaction?"

I'd thought I would die. I'd thought Callum had abandoned and betrayed me. And then there'd been gunshots and a shower of glass, and the man who'd wanted me dead had blown apart and landed in pieces at my feet. I'd known Callum had that violence in him, and I'd craved it. He'd used it to save me, and the night before he'd controlled it to give me what I needed so desperately.

"I wanted you from the beginning." It was too honest, but I'd been stripped bare, in more ways than one. I felt like all my nerves lay on the surface, flayed and exposed.

Callum held my gaze with his own, dark and steady. He didn't hesitate. "So did I."

As I stared at him, dumbfounded, he rose up and took my face between his hands. Callum had such large, rough hands, with long callused fingers. Not gentle hands, not soft hands. The tools of a killer. He stroked his thumbs over the corners of my lips, his fingers buried in my hair.

When he leaned in, his mouth met mine in a kiss so sweet and chaste it made me ache. A brush of the lips, so delicate I nearly couldn't feel it.

Except that every part of me felt it, down to my toes.

"I'm too tired to help clean us up," I whispered against his mouth, and felt him smile.

I knew how ridiculous it sounded. He'd run to the villa, broken into the garden, killed our enemy and then gotten blasted with magic so hard he nearly died.

And I was the one who claimed to be too tired to lift a washcloth.

"I know," he said simply. And he finished cleaning me, rising a couple of times to rinse out the cloth, my sweat and the blood from my split lip and all the dirt of travel trickling away.

I leaned back and watched as Callum efficiently stripped his own clothes, setting his guns carefully on the marble vanity table. His torso offered me a map to his history, the faded, overlapping scars of so many brushes with death. Lean muscles, like a panther, all coiled power and ruthlessly suppressed violence. As he swiped the cloth over his own body, I wished I had the energy to trace its path with my tongue, taste the marks that his life had left on him. His pants came off next, and my fingers clenched around the edge of the chair. Ancestors, but he was a work of art. Not a painting, or a sculpture, but a charcoal sketch by an artist of incomparable talent, rough lines and motions translating to something exquisite. He dropped his boxers and rinsed out the cloth again to wash below the waist, and then I couldn't look at anything but his cock. Now *that* was perfect.

Callum dropped the cloth on the sink and turned, totally and unselfconsciously naked, to pull me up and out of the chair. I moaned as he pressed me against him, finally with nothing between us. I wanted to rub against him like a cat, but he half-carried me back into the bedroom and slid me between the sheets of the bed before I could do more than hold on.

He disappeared into the bath and returned a moment later with a small bottle in his hand and a light in his eyes I couldn't possibly misinterpret. When he climbed in, I spread my legs and pulled him down, into my arms and into my kiss.

Callum didn't speak, but he didn't need to. Every touch showed me that I was precious, that I had value—at least in that moment, and at least to him. It couldn't have been more different from the night before: slow and careful instead of rough and brutal. But I'd needed that the night before, craved it. Today, I needed what he gave me.

I tipped my head back to let him lick a path down my throat, my eyes fluttering closed, and stroked my hands down his back, feeling the play of muscles there. If we had all the time in the world to explore one another, would it always be like this, and like the night before? Callum expertly reading me, knowing precisely what I needed, and giving it to me without hesitation?

He moved in me with measured, controlled thrusts, a hand buried in my hair. His teeth caught at my shoulder and then his lips found my cheek, kissing me and breathing me in.

When I finished, it felt more like the tide rolling out than the frantic explosion of the night before. All in a rush, what little strength I had flowed away. Callum pulled out of me but didn't go anywhere, enclosing me in his arms and tucking me under the blankets, safe at last. I fell asleep with our hands wrapped together, pressed against my heart.

Callum

Linden had been asleep for a solid hour before I dared to stir.

Well, before I forced myself to stir, at least. I didn't want to leave. Real life seemed very fucking far away, and even more unappealing. I had Linden wrapped up so tightly that I could hardly tell whose legs were whose, all tangled together. I'd wanted this the night before, to have him in a real bed. Safe. Cozy. Unafraid.

I had it, and now I had to leave it. Leave him. No fucking

choice in the matter, because Evalt might be dead, and all the problems he'd caused in this realm on their way to being solved, but the same couldn't be said for my own world. Had he put the spooks under the same compulsion he'd used on his soldiers here? Possibly, and if so, that magic would've broken at the same time. There might be a couple of incredibly fucking confused CIA assholes sitting in a cubicle somewhere, blinking out of what felt like a dream and wondering why they'd abandoned all their paperwork to chase some two-bit hitman and his handler around. I hoped they got burned for it, but I couldn't count on it. Evalt might've used some good old-fashioned non-magical compulsion, like a large untraceable wire transfer. That would stay operational long after he'd died.

I needed to go home.

Pulling my fingers out from between Linden's felt like the heaviest lift I'd ever had. Long and slender, they slid between mine like silk, and their absence made my hand feel empty. I rolled away from him, from the soft swell of his ass nestled into my groin, from the length of his elegant back pressed to my chest, from the lightness of his hair tickling my nose. I pressed a single kiss to the point of his shoulder and then covered him with the blankets all the way up to his neck.

With the efficiency of long practice getting the hell out of places quickly, I dressed and got my holsters in place and tiptoed out of the room, shutting the door behind me silently and forcing myself not to look back.

The house had come back to life in the couple of hours I'd spent locked away with Linden, with servants in the halls busy on errands I couldn't guess at, and the sounds of a household putting itself in order echoing in the distance. I asked the first person I passed, I guessed a housemaid by her apron and air of being incredibly busy, where to find Lady Lisandra, and received a curtsey and directions to her study.

A few hallways and random staircases later, and I knocked

at a door that had been polished carefully enough to show me my own reflection, albeit muted and distorted by the grain of the wood. I looked away. I didn't feel like looking myself in the eye.

Lady Lisandra called to me to come in, and I did, closing the door behind me. The room held a desk, a few chairs set around a low table, and a set of bookshelves against the wall. One of the wide glass doors I'd passed on the terrace looked out over a particularly bright section of flowerbeds. The sun had begun to set, and everything held a weird, reddish tint. I'd never get used to this place. The only other light in the room came from two off-white globes suspended from the ceiling.

Lady Lisandra rose from the chair behind the desk as I entered, bowing her head in a way I knew had to be precisely calculated and that there was no way I'd be able to understand or duplicate. I settled for a nod, and she came around the desk, waving me to one of the velvet-and-gold chairs by the table. I lowered myself into it awkwardly, afraid to break it.

She sat opposite, leaning back with a sigh. She didn't look like she'd been a hostage earlier in the day. From the top of her perfectly braided dark hair to her immaculate blue dress to the tips of her velvet-slippered feet, she had me outclassed in every possible way.

"I had thought I might see you sooner than later, Lord Callum," she said. "You don't seem like a man who rests when he has unfinished business."

Unfinished business. Like the sleeping beauty upstairs, who didn't know he'd be alone when he woke up. I forced myself not to fidget and kept my face blank. "Says the woman who's working in her office instead of resting in her own bed. You've had quite a day yourself, ma'am." She acknowledged it with a shrug and a half-smile. "By the way, I'm not Lord Callum anymore, if I ever was."

She raised her eyebrows. "Oh?"

"Lord Linden bested me in single combat. I surrendered and

everything."

Lady Lisandra stared at me for a moment, and then she burst into laughter, high and bright and musical, her green eyes glittering. If I hadn't just left the loveliest thing I'd ever touched in a bed upstairs, she would've had me on my knees.

"Oh, ancestors," she said at last, through her giggles, "I needed that. I presume Lord Linden was not the instigator of this...combat?"

"He wasn't. But he seemed happy enough to hit me." I hadn't meant to say that, and I shifted uneasily in my chair. It'd been made for someone about half my size, and it creaked under me. "Anyway. The title's his. And the lands. And whatever else. If you feel like you owe me a favor, I'd appreciate it if you made sure he got to keep it."

Lady Lisandra eyed me thoughtfully, tapping her fingers on the arm of her chair. "I owe you a much larger favor than that, Callum. My life and the lives of everyone under my protection are worth more to me than handling a simple matter I'd have seen to in any case for Linden's sake. But since you're leaving Lord Linden's affairs to me, I presume you are also leaving for your own realm."

She didn't sound like she approved, but I didn't need her permission. Did she know how things were, between me and Linden? I'd bet on yes. She seemed way too fucking observant for comfort. Great, someone else who'd think I was a callous asshole. Not that I needed another, but I sure seemed to collect them.

"If the favor you owe me includes getting me there, then yeah, I'm going back. I do have unfinished business." She made a 'go on' gesture, and so I did, telling her briefly how I'd ended up meeting Linden in the first place. Admitting I'd originally meant to kill him made me feel like vermin, but she didn't seem like someone who put a lot of value on moral judgments over practical results. "So I need to find Jesse, if he's even still alive," I finished. "And make sure whoever Evalt had working for him over there isn't going to be a problem anymore."

Lady Lisandra tapped a finger against her lips, *hmm*ing in thought. "I very much doubt they will be," she said at last. "This assassin—the one you believe to have been from this realm?" I nodded. "He would have been an absolute last resort. We have laws prohibiting us from acting against one another while in other realms than our own. Those places are neutral ground. We conduct business meetings in your restaurants sometimes for that reason." Well, that explained some of the weirder shit I'd seen in New York steakhouses. "The laws are strict. The High Court would have acted to subdue Evalt immediately had they discovered he'd sent one of our own to kill another one of our own in the human realm, and using human intermediaries, while possibly a gray area, would still have garnered him attention he didn't want from the Queen."

"That still doesn't reassure me much. Okay, so your queen or your court would've killed Evalt before I had to if they'd known. But apparently they didn't. That doesn't help me." Knowing this realm's authorities had the power to put Evalt down like a dog, but hadn't done it, actually pissed me off more than anything had in years. I didn't say it, but my tone said it clearly enough.

Lady Lisandra nodded and sighed. "I don't disagree, although the point is now moot. However, you know Evalt used compulsion on his servants. He had very little else in his arsenal, when it came to attracting followers."

"You mean he couldn't rely on his charming personality?"

She dimpled a smile. "Indeed. And his knowledge of the human realm was very limited, one reason why I chose to send Linden—I beg your pardon, *Lord* Linden—there when I realized his life might be in imminent danger. Evalt would not have known how to extract assistance or obedience from someone in your world through any other means. And he wouldn't have known whom to use, not exactly. He probably found one relatively powerful man, someone he could access without too much trouble. A politician, a wealthy businessman. Evalt would have compelled him, and then left the details to that man. Your…'spooks'…were merely following orders from some superior, orders that will now be rescinded."

I let out a long breath. "How sure are you about this? Your analysis of the situation?"

"Very nearly certain," she said. "I've known Evalt for many, many years. And my understanding of the human realm far surpassed his."

"I hope you're right. I still need to go back and see for myself."

"I understand." She rose and went behind her desk, opening a small cabinet set against the wall. From it, she withdrew a green glass prism, that cast odd blue refractions even though I couldn't see any direct light hitting it. She set it on her desk and beckoned me over.

Fucking great. More magic. "This won't take me through that shitty labyrinth, will it?"

"No, the journey will be direct. You'll go to the same place I sent Linden, unless you require a specific destination. Readjusting the focus will take time, however, if you need me to do so."

I had a car in that crappy little town, if it hadn't gotten towed. And I could always steal another, anyway. And a phone. I might even buy one if I arrived during the day. "Sure. That works."

"Place your hands on it, then, and be ready."

Right that second. Right that second, I was leaving. And all of a sudden, I couldn't quite do it.

Unfinished business. Fuck.

"Will you tell your cousins goodbye for me? Kaspar and Oskar. And—" I swallowed hard. "And Linden—"

"You haven't said your farewells to Linden?" she demanded sharply. "Where is he?"

I felt like pond scum under her cold gaze. "Asleep."

Her lip curled. "I will *not* pass a message to him. Do you

know that I was there when he was born?" Fuck, she didn't look old enough for that. I shook my head. *Lower* than pond scum. "I held him while his mother rested from her labor. He played under this desk as a child, hiding from Kaspar. I used to let him brush my hair while I sang to him. He is not my child, Callum, but near enough. And I will not be the messenger of your...I hesitate to use the word cowardice, after your other actions today. But."

"But if the shoe fits," I muttered.

"If I understand your idiom, yes," she snapped. "If Linden is distressed by your abrupt departure, that is your responsibility alone. I will urge him to forget you, but I won't speak for you. I will tell my cousins you have gone, and that you send your regards. You didn't leave *them* asleep and sneak out like a thief in the night."

My throat felt too tight, but I forced myself to reply. "Thank you." I couldn't find anything else to say. She tilted her head, as if to tell me, *Well, get on with it.* I laid my hands on the crystal thing.

A gut-churning, time-twisting moment later, and Lady Lisandra's magic spat me out hard. I landed on my hands and knees on something dark, damp, and chilly.

Sand. I sifted a handful through my fingers. And the sound of waves to my right. The cold caress of fog against my burning face.

Right back where I'd started.

Wearily, with something I couldn't allow myself to recognize as bitter regret burning in the pit of my stomach, I got to my feet and headed for town to find a car, a phone, and a fucking drink.

Chapter Eighteen

Callum

Finding Jesse turned out to be a lot easier than convincing him I hadn't had a psychotic break.

I stole a phone out of a purse—at the Cannibal Bean, of course, and seeing some guy who wasn't Linden behind the counter nearly broke me—and headed down the alley to find a car to steal. I'd ditched the idea of going back for the rental car or for anything I'd left behind in the motel room. Too much chance of a trap there, if Evalt's magic hadn't burned out the way Lady Lisandra thought.

I texted Jesse's burner phone on the way, a phone that stayed turned off and out of sight until something like this came up.

By the time I'd stolen a nondescript sedan, Jesse had responded, his coded message the right match to mine. We did a couple more back-and-forths, and then my stolen phone rang right as I pulled out of town and onto the little two-lane highway. I poked the speaker button.

"Where the fuck are you?" Jesse sounded like he'd hit the end of his patience a long way back and kept on going full-speed. "I tried your burner. Tried all the usual—you dropped off the face of the earth."

Jesse cursed at me as I laughed, helplessly, unable to hold it back no matter how hard I tried. "Sorry," I choked. "Sorry. Really, really fucking crazy few days, and you have no idea how you hit the nail on the head there. I'm in California. What's the sitrep? Because I really have been off the grid. You seriously have no idea."

"You're going to be giving me an idea," Jesse growled. Jesus, he was usually the soft-spoken one in our little duo. He'd really been worried. I knew I gave a fuck about him, but sometimes I'd wondered if the opposite held true. "I've had a couple of my old contacts checking up on things. It looks like we might be in the clear, as of this morning. I'm waiting for confirmation. In the meantime, head for Idaho."

The line went dead.

I stopped for coffee and gas, and then more coffee, and I hit the Idaho border twelve hours later, just as the sun started to slant down behind me.

Another call, and Jesse confirmed we weren't on the run anymore, as far as he knew. And he gave me a location about another two hours away.

I stopped for more coffee at another gas station, even though the coffee sucked, because I couldn't fucking handle ordering from some guy in a coffee shop. Every contact I had with another human being felt disjointed, off, like I'd left some part of myself I couldn't function without in the other realm. How could less than a week make my own world feel so alien? How could I care enough about someone I'd only known...I shoved that thought aside with extreme prejudice. Introspection never led anywhere good.

I finally pulled up in front of a cabin outside a tiny little nowhere town as the sun set.

Jesse stood on the porch waiting for me, and the sight of his sandy mop of hair and broad grin nearly did me in. He waved with his prosthetic arm and flipped me off with his real hand.

I had to sit in the car for a second to get my shit together.

Fucking Christ, I'd turned into a sap.

Half an hour later, we sat at the cabin's ancient Formica kitchen table, both with a neat bourbon. A third neat bourbon in my case, because I'd known I'd need a few to tell him my side of the story.

Jesse glared at me, hazel eyes narrowed. "They drugged you," he said. "Callum, whatever you were on, there might be traces of it left. A full work-up—"

"I wasn't drugged." Even though that'd been my first thought too, a few days slash ten years ago. "I'm sane. As sane as I was before, asshole, don't say a fucking word."

Jesse chuckled and took a swig of his drink. "I didn't need to. But come on. Fairyland?"

"It wasn't like you're making it sound, no glittery wings or wands or any bullshit like that. But it wasn't the normal world. Wherever we were, the moon and the stars were different. It couldn't have been normal Earth."

He drained the rest of his glass and set it down with a loud clink. "You were drugged."

I opened my mouth to argue, but…what the fuck did it matter if he believed me, in the end? I didn't have any proof. It hadn't crossed my mind to try to bring any back with me. I'd assumed, stupidly, that Jesse would take my word for it, because—I guess because he was the only person in the world I gave a fuck about, and that's what you did for people you maybe liked, right? You trusted them.

If Jesse had told me the same story, I'd have poured him another drink, just as Jesse was doing for me now, and told him he'd been drugged.

The only problem was, now I'd been to two worlds.

And there were people I gave a fuck about in the other one.

"Sure," I said at last, after a long, long couple of minutes of staring down into my bourbon, watching the light of the single bare bulb on the ceiling glimmer in the liquor in little streaks of white reflection. "I probably was."

A long, heavy sigh was my only answer. I drank up. And then drank up again.

At some point, I drained the last few drops, looked at the bottle, found it empty, and pushed my chair back from the table. I hadn't eaten in a while. Was I hungry? No, not really.

I felt empty, but it wasn't food I needed.

"I'm sacking out," I told Jesse, who frowned at me worriedly, and I went into the cabin's small living room to collapse on the couch. The place only had one bedroom, and he'd gotten there first.

I lay with my arm over my eyes and tracked his movements by the sounds, first hitting the kitchen light switch, and then checking the door and windows, and then finally walking by on his way to bed.

The last light turned off, and I didn't have anything else to focus on.

I should never have come back. I'd been shoving the thought away through the whole drive across the width of California and Nevada.

Jesse had already been safe. I'd made sure of that when I shoved that flashlight into Evalt's brain. He'd never have known what happened to me, but would he have cared that much, really? He'd have cared. I knew that. But he'd have moved on, like men in our line of work had to do often enough when colleagues and friends got themselves killed or vanished without a trace. I had more than a few ghosts like that in my past. Guys I'd fought with, guys I would've killed or died for—for a while. Until they faded away, and I moved on.

I hadn't even asked Lady Lisandra about what it'd take to go back. I'd been so fixated on getting home, getting back to normality, that I hadn't stopped to consider that I didn't have to. My whole adult life I'd never seen it, the possibility of another option than focusing on the immediate goal, and then resting up just enough to tackle the next.

What the fuck was normality to me? And why the fuck would I want to rush back to it? Another motel room, another file, another bullet in someone's head? It had its moments. And it paid a lot better than washing dishes in the back of a diner, the only other job I actually qualified for, but I never bothered to spend the money on anything. Yeah. I could retire right now, at thirty-four. Fucking great. And do what?

My fists clenched as Linden's face, his smile, popped back into my mind, like it'd been doing all fucking day.

It seemed simple now, lying on a musty-smelling couch in the ass-end of Idaho, of all fucking places. I'd had a choice, but I hadn't realized it. And now the only choice that mattered to me didn't exist anymore.

Maybe I should try to pretend it *had* all been a drug-induced hallucination. That way I wouldn't have to look my own stupidity and blindness in the face. Linden's throat under my hand, and the light in his eyes when I kissed him, and the warmth of his slender body pressed up against me, all trusting and sleepy...all a hallucination.

I slept that night because my body had hit a point where it wouldn't do anything else, but I woke often, on that tipping point where the worst thoughts in my head bled into even worse dreams.

When the sun came up and filtered its way through the old, mildewy curtains at the front of the cabin, it found me staring at the dusty ceiling, trying to figure out if any of the spiderwebs were less than twenty years old.

Jesse hadn't stirred. Outside the cabin, some birds chirped. The wind rustled and bumped a tree branch against the eaves of the roof over the kitchen.

Muted male voices rose over it, just for a second.

I had my reloaded Beretta in hand by the time I rolled silently onto the floor another half-second later. Maybe we weren't as in the clear as Jesse's contacts had thought. Or maybe some hikers had wandered through, but I wasn't taking any chances.

"Jesse," I hissed through the cracked bedroom door. "Company."

His blankets rustled, and I knew he'd be right behind me and armed. I crab-walked across the room and carefully lined up an eye with the tiny gap in the curtains over the front window.

Two men stood in front of the cabin. One had his back to me, tall and broad enough to double as a brick wall, with long black hair waving down over his leather armor. He'd left the sword at home, and even from behind I could tell from the stiffness in his shoulders that he regretted it.

The other had dark hair, and that was all I could see...but I didn't need to see any more than that.

My forehead thunked against the windowsill as I slumped there, breathing heavily, my eyes squeezed shut. I'd never thought I'd see Oskar or Kaspar again. A few days before, meeting them in the labyrinth, I'd have assumed I'd never want to.

Jesse's whisper of my name brought me out of it. I turned my head to find him crouched behind me, his gun at the ready. "Are you all right?"

"Yep," I said, not bothering to keep my voice down. "And there's someone outside I need you to meet."

When I flung the door open, they stood looking up at me from just in front of the porch steps. "The location spell worked," Oskar said, with a note of surprise—and in English. Apparently they'd taken the time to have Lady Lisandra help them with a spell-cake.

"I told you it would." Kaspar sounded smug. "Evalt's magical residue is extremely distinctive."

Jesse crowded into the doorway next to me, peering over my shoulder. "Whose fucking *what*?"

Oskar and Kaspar might've left their swords and light-staffs in their own realm, but they weren't blending in, not even a little bit. Oskar's leather armor, Kaspar's dress-thing and giant boots...yeah, they looked like they'd escaped from a Renaissance Faire. Or maybe a psych ward.

"I wasn't drugged," I said, turning enough to see and savor the look of total confusion on Jesse's face. "Oskar, Kaspar, this is my partner Jesse. Jesse, Oskar and Kaspar. They're fairies."

And then I lost it and leaned against the door frame shaking with laughter, relief welling up so strongly I almost couldn't take it, while they all stared at me with matching offended looks on their faces.

"I can't believe you!" Oskar shouted. "Laughing? After the way you left?" He charged at me, only to come up short as Jesse pointed his cocked pistol right at Oskar's chest. Oskar went red, murder on his face. "You'll hide behind him? You fucking coward."

"No, not hiding," I said. I pushed down on Jesse's arm. "Gun away. We're all friends here. Oskar's probably going to punch me, but I have it coming."

"We're both going to punch you," Kaspar put in. He'd crossed his arms so that he could glare at me more effectively, and the mannerism reminded me so strongly of Linden that my chest clenched.

Linden. "Does he know you're here?" I didn't even need to say his name. They'd both know exactly who I meant.

"No," Oskar growled. "We didn't want to upset him."

"Upset him more," Kaspar added pointedly.

"Are you all insane, or am I?" Jesse demanded. He'd lowered the gun, at least, but the tension in his body hadn't diminished. "Does who know? This Evalt person?"

"I told you about Evalt," I said wearily. "Remember? Purple sparks, wanted to kill everyone, hired the spooks, I iced him with a flashlight, yadda yadda. No. Linden."

"The target," Jesse said evenly. Suspiciously so. "The one you ended up helping."

Oskar went from red to purple, and I winced as he opened his mouth. Nope, maybe I hadn't told Jesse everything, and I didn't need Oskar doing the explaining. "More than a target," I said quietly, and looked Jesse in the eyes, knowing he'd understand.

He did. "Ah," he said, on a long, blown-out breath. "And these guys are…?"

"Linden's childhood friends."

Jesse's lips quirked, and the tension bled out of him at last, his gun arm coming all the way down to hang at his side, relaxed. "So you went to—this place. Seduced their best friend, after almost killing him. And ran out on him. And now they're here to beat the shit out of you?"

I winced, but I couldn't deny it. Jesse sighed again, and he turned to Oskar.

"Fair enough. Have at it, guys," he said. "I'll go make some coffee."

When I looked back at Oskar, he was gaping like a fish, all the wind out of his big and angry sails. "Okay, you heard the man," I said, and safetied the Beretta, holding my arms out at my sides. "Have at it. One free punch each. Then I hit back."

Slowly, slowly, the too-bright color in Oskar's face faded away, leaving him back to his usual ruddy-tan. He eyed me thoughtfully. "What are your intentions with regard to Linden?"

My intentions. Trust Oskar to sound like he'd stepped right out of a BBC movie.

I didn't have any intentions. I just knew that lying on an ancient, ratty couch in an Idaho safehouse with a gun two inches from my hand was more or less what I had to look forward to here in my own realm. Or I could spend some of my savings and live on a beach somewhere, getting drunk and fucking tourists.

Or I could have a life that meant something to me, and possibly even to someone else.

"I'm coming back with you," I said, and felt the rightness of it. "Linden's going to be a lord now, and from what I've seen, that's not necessarily a guarantee of safety in your world. He'll need a bodyguard, right? Or something like that. I can protect him. I won't leave him alone unless he tells me that's what he wants." And maybe not even then. He'd have to be incredibly fucking convincing. I didn't bother to say that part.

That didn't really answer Oskar's question. I wasn't sure I could answer Oskar's question. It seemed like something only Linden had the right to ask, and God knew if he'd even want an answer to it after the way I'd run out on him.

"Fine," Oskar said after a moment. "But I'm still taking that free punch. I hope your jaw's as sturdy as it looks."

My lips twitched upward, and it felt so fucking good after a night of feeling like I might never smile again.

"Okay," I said. "Give it your best shot. And then let's get going."

Chapter Nineteen

Callum

Lady Lisandra threw a ball in Linden's honor three days after we got back—maybe not coincidentally, with exactly the right timing for my bruised jaw to heal up completely. And thank God for their realm's sophistry when it came to the rules of single combat, because if not for that the ball might've been in *my* honor. I'd rather have gone back to Afghanistan. Naked, and armed only with a flashlight.

It wasn't only *their* realm anymore, though, and that'd take some getting used to. Our realm. Mine and Linden's.

And Jesse's now, too. I'd grabbed a spot propping up the exterior wall at the southeastern corner of the ballroom, where I had a clear line of sight to each of the glass doors and also the huge double doors leading into the hall. Even though the room had filled to bursting with weird people in elaborate clothing sipping multi-colored liquors I couldn't begin to name, I had a view of him standing by one of the doors to the terrace, leaning down to hear Lady Lisandra as she said something for his ears only.

She had a hand on his arm, and a flirtatious smile on her face, and I had no doubt Jesse was about to enjoy the rest of his night—or what was left of it, anyway, since this party had lasted for fucking endless hours already and it had to be close to four in the morning. Jesse looked somewhere between overjoyed and stunned, which seemed about right for someone in Lady Lisandra's crosshairs.

When I'd told him I meant to go back with Oskar and Kaspar, it'd taken him thirty seconds to mull it over, shrug, and tell me someone had to watch my back—and since he'd been doing it for six years, why stop now? Jesse didn't have anyone back home any more than I did, and he'd joined the Air Force originally out of insatiable curiosity. It made sense. And it removed the one regret I'd had about leaving. We'd taken half an hour to pack up all the weaponry and ammo Jesse had stored at the cabin, and then we'd gone without looking back.

Even if he'd already been happy enough with the idea of a new adventure, he hadn't counted on stepping out of the magic portal Lady Lisandra had sent to collect us and immediately meeting the hottest woman in two worlds, who wanted to dress him in fancy clothes, get him drunk, and probably seduce him. He'd muttered something to me about winning the lottery, fist-bumped me, and run with it.

I scanned the room again, looking for Linden this time. I'd taken a quick circuit of the perimeter a few minutes before, leaving him bowing and being bowed to by all the important people who'd come to be important at him. Honestly, I'd done my walk-around more because I couldn't get near him than because I'd been worried about security.

Anyway, he'd gotten lost in the crowd somewhere, and I was trying not to sulk too obviously.

I slid my hand under the jacket Silvi had wrestled me into earlier, making sure my Beretta sat loose and easy. The jacket had about ten pounds of silver embroidery on it, and weird points on the collar that kept poking me under my chin, but it hid a holster. I could live with it.

Linden's outfit made mine look plain, with all kinds of

flowing blue silk and fancy gold buttons and honest-to-fucking-God stockings underneath. Of course, most of the people here were wearing stockings. I'd drawn the line there, and had black pants and boots.

Not that I had any problem with Linden's stockings. I'd been fantasizing about how I'd want to take them off ever since he put them on, and that wasn't because I didn't like them.

If I ever even got the chance to touch him, let alone try to undress him.

Because Linden hadn't exactly been giving me a green light to undress him over the past few days.

Strike that. I'd gotten a red light on so much as speaking to him.

He'd been there when Jesse and I came through the portal, hanging back behind Lady Lisandra and watching solemnly as we stepped out. He'd looked at me—one long, unreadable look. He hadn't said a word to me. He'd quietly introduced himself to Jesse, and then he'd taken Kaspar by the arm and walked away, leaving me staring after him with a hard, cold lump of misery in my gut.

I deserved it. Fuck, did I deserve it.

But every damn time I'd tried to get him alone and talk over the past few days, we'd seemed to 'accidentally' get interrupted by someone who needed one of us to do something right that minute.

Try on a jacket. Write a polite note to someone who'd congratulated Linden on his new title and wealth. See a visitor, give an opinion on something in the kitchen, and so on and on and on.

Actually, all of those were things they needed Linden to do. No one seemed to need me to do anything except pace the halls and wait for thirty seconds of Linden's time. Which I didn't ever seem to get. Even when no one interrupted us, he always managed to think of somewhere he needed to be, dashing off with a fake half-smile and without meeting my eyes.

I'd have tried to track him down at night, but I'd been bunked down with Oskar, Kaspar, and Jesse in a sort of bachelor barracks, and I had no idea where Linden slept. It would've been an easy enough thing to find out, except that if Linden wanted me to know…sneaking up on him in the middle of the night like the assassin I was trying not to be anymore felt fucking wrong.

I missed him, though, a down-deep ache that I couldn't ignore.

And I'd started to wonder if I'd missed my chance completely. If I'd spend the rest of my life trailing around after him at parties like this, armed to the teeth and scaring the guests. Aching for him, and never allowed to touch.

I caught a flash of blue silk and a glimpse of the brightest smile in the room and zeroed in.

There he was. And that tall, handsome guy talking to him had leaned in way too fucking close.

I'd sworn to myself I'd stay out of the way, lurk against the wall, and let Linden do his lord of the realm thing. I didn't have any official status here. Yeah, I'd killed Evalt, which gave me a certain level of reputation…but it was the kind of reputation that made people side-eye you and shuffle out of reach, not offer you a glass of rainbow liquor and try to be your friend.

I didn't have any official status in Linden's life, either. I wished I could've had a few hours alone with some of that liquor, because then at least I could've brooded about it drunk instead of stone-cold, miserably sober.

No time for brooding, though. The tall guy put his hand on Linden's arm, thumb rubbing over the curve of Linden's shoulder, and I'd pushed off from the wall and into the crowd before I'd even made a conscious decision.

A path appeared before me like magic, no one wanting a flashlight through the eye, I was guessing, and it only took me a minute to get across the room. By the time I did, the too-handsome asshole had Linden's hand in his, and he'd gotten close enough to start angling for a kiss.

Linden saw me coming over the guy's shoulder, and his eyes went wide. "You should probably stop touching me," I heard him hiss under his breath.

My fists clenched at my sides. Why hadn't he told the fucker to get his hands off before I came along, if he didn't want to be touched like that? *Did* he want to be touched like that by someone else? Was it only getting caught he cared about, because he thought I'd, what, hurt *him* if I caught him with another guy?

I pushed past the guy and turned to stand shoulder to shoulder with Linden. "Hi," I said.

And it was all I needed to say. The fucker scuttled off into the crowd without a word, dropping Linden's hand like it'd gone white-hot.

When I got done staring a hole into the back of his head, I turned to Linden, not sure what to expect.

The look in his eyes nearly had me on my knees. I'd thought Lady Lisandra held the gold medal for eye-fucking a guy into submission, but Linden managed it with no more than one glance at me from under his lashes.

Okay, fucking enough. Enough of this ball, enough of other people thinking they could put their hands all over him, and enough of not having touched or even really spoken to him for *three fucking days*.

"Let's get some air," I growled into his ear. I felt his shiver where his shoulder brushed mine.

"Why don't you escort me to the gardens," Linden said, in a strange, strained tone that could've meant anything from *And then you can fuck right off* to *And then you can fuck me against a wall*.

My heart raced, and I all I could do was nod. He set his hand in the crook of my elbow, and the simple touch felt like it burned through my jacket and shirt and all the way down to the bone. A couple of knots of revelers looked like they meant to start chatting away at Linden, but two scowls cleared a path, and I whisked him out through the glass doors in the farthest corner of the ballroom and onto the terrace.

More people stood out here, laughing and drinking, the bright feathers in their hair bobbing and their silk robes swishing as they gesticulated.

Hugging the wall, and keeping Linden between me and it just in case, I strode down the terrace as quickly as possible without looking like we were running away. I glanced around, evaluating the options. The garden had a lot of nooks and crannies. Of course, the gardens were also open to the party, and I had no idea which of the plants might come alive at night...but presumably Linden did. I towed him down the farthest set of stairs at the end of the terrace and along a path between flowerbeds.

"This way," Linden said. I let him tow me in turn, past a huge flowering bush and a fountain, and then down another path.

Linden tugged my arm, pulling me toward what looked like a tall, impenetrable hedge. "What—" And then he let go of my arm, dodged to the side, and vanished into thin air, leaving me gaping.

His head popped out of a gap in the hedge, which wasn't impenetrable after all: it had two overlapping layers, and a hidden space in between just large enough to fit through. His golden hair gleamed white in the fading moonlight.

When I squeezed through, I found myself in a little—room, really, with walls made out of hedge and a partial roof of flowery branches. A carpet of soft grass dotted with tiny flowers that shone in the dark like stars spread out under my feet.

And Linden stood in the middle, fidgeting with his hands in front of him like he'd suddenly gotten hit with an attack of nerves.

"Kaspar and I used to hide here when we didn't want to study our history books," Linden said, his voice hushed.

Maybe that would've been exactly the kind of thing I'd have wanted to know about Linden if I'd spent the last three days sleeping in his bed and spending time with him during the day, but right now the detail just irritated me. I hadn't come out here with him to get distracted by childhood anecdotes.

"Why haven't I seen you since we got back?" It came out too harsh, too demanding.

"You've seen me every day."

"Linden."

He stared down at his hands, twisting and twisting them around each other. "I didn't know what you wanted from me."

I closed the distance between us in two quick strides, stopping a foot from him, close enough to breathe him in. Close enough that he had to tip his head down and away to avoid looking into my eyes, baring the slightest curve of the side of his throat to me. A little gust of breeze drifted by and tangled a strand of his hair at his temple.

That did me in.

I caught his chin in my hand, tipping his head up until he had to look at me, brushing that tendril of hair away with my other hand and then cupping his cheek, framing his beautiful face. "I came back," I said. "That ought to make it pretty goddamn clear what I want."

"I woke up alone, Callum." For all his avoidance before, he'd found the courage to stare me down now, and I felt like the one who ought to look away. I couldn't, though. He had me. "When I went downstairs, you were already gone."

"I had to get back to find Jesse, make sure he'd made it somewhere safe. Make sure no one was still after him."

"I understand that," Linden said slowly. "But you could have told me that. You could have—Lady Lisandra said you'd made no arrangements to return. You didn't even leave a message for me."

Because she wouldn't let me. True enough as far as it went, but I bit the words back. She'd been right not to, and Linden didn't deserve a bunch of bullshit excuses anyway, especially not with the raw, miserable hurt in his voice and in his beautiful face.

He'd avoided me, and he'd had every right to. And now I had one more chance, maybe, to convince him to change his mind.

"It didn't even occur to me that I had a choice until I'd already made it, and it was too late," I said, my words halting and hoarse. My turn to swallow, my throat painfully dry. Fuck. Linden was right. Humans did lie a fuck of a lot, and I lied more than most. Why did honesty have to feel like ripping out a fistful of my internal organs and tossing them in the dirt at Linden's feet? "I have—had—a life. I'm used to it. I guess the plan was kind of—to make enough money and retire. Except I already did the first part. I think I couldn't imagine doing anything but what I was doing, until I ran into someone who did it better and took one too many bullets. Like—like fate. I thought I'd never see you—"

My voice broke, right as the look in his eyes broke me. Confusion, and hope, and lingering anger. Betrayal. I slid my hands down to his shoulders, and then lower, sweeping them over his back, my fingers snagging the delicate silk of his clothing. I had to feel him. Words didn't work well for me. I could—God, all the things I wanted to tell him would be so much easier if I could do it with my body, but I'd done that already.

And then left him.

No wonder he felt betrayed.

"Oskar punched me in the jaw," I said at last. "Before we came back from my realm. I deserved it. You could too, you know? Maybe that'd help."

The joke didn't land, and I didn't even get a smile.

"No need," he said flatly. "I already defeated you in single combat, remember?"

He'd defeated me in every possible way, he just didn't know it yet, and I couldn't seem to figure out how the fuck to tell him. I wasn't sure if he'd want to keep the spoils of victory, though. I wasn't much of a prize, unless you needed someone to kill an evil sorcerer with random plastic objects.

"Yeah," I said softly. "Yeah, you did. Tough guy."

Finally, the corners of his lips quirked. "Not tough enough to do what I probably ought to do, and tell you to stop touching me."

I felt like all my blood stopped flowing for a second, congealed into something frozen and deathly. "Please don't." The words tore out of me and left me bleeding. "God, Linden. Please don't. Even if that's what I deserve."

And then my throat tightened too much, and nothing else came out. My arms had locked around him, probably squeezing him too hard for comfort, and I wasn't sure I could let him go again.

Linden looked at me long and hard. Making up his mind, I thought. And then he nodded once.

"You gave me your word once before," he said softly. "Promised me you wouldn't hurt me. I believed you. Now promise me again, only this time I want your word you won't leave me again. Not without a good reason, and not without telling me first."

My breath came out in a rush, my heart pounding from the effort of holding the air in my lungs too long, and my head spun. I couldn't see anything but his shining eyes. "I can't imagine a reason good enough for leaving you. And yes," I added. "I promise. I fucking swear on anything you can think of."

At last, at last, Linden touched me, sliding his hands up my abdomen and chest, his fingers exploring. Teasing. Tentative.

"I was so glad when you finally came and found me tonight," he said in a soft rush.

Even in the washed-out moonlight, his eyes shone a pure blue, a blue I'd have picked out of any lineup of colors anywhere. He looked like a dream. Like a crack in the normal world, or what passed for normal here, had broken open to let in sunlight too bright and too beautiful for human eyes. Even in the dark, he was drenched in sunlight.

"I'm sorry I didn't do this the second I came back," I said, and kissed him, trying to put everything I couldn't find the words for into the press of my mouth on his. I expected him to be hesitant, to make me work for it.

Anything but melt into me like I'd cut his strings and open

his mouth for me with a low moan that went all the way down my spine. I wrapped him in my arms and kissed him until I couldn't breathe and he was gasping against my lips.

When he pulled me down onto the grass without a word, I followed, covering him with my bigger body and caging him in with my arms. He tipped his head back, showing me what he wanted.

I wanted to give him what he wanted, always. The pulse in his throat quivered under my tongue, and his clothes gave way to my hands. I stripped him until he didn't have anything but those silk stockings and a little wisp of silk above that was what passed for boxers in this realm, I guessed.

No complaints from me. His cock stood up to greet me, outlined in pale blue silk, a little darker patch spreading where he'd started to get wet for me. I traced the tip of his cock with my tongue and made him moan and arch up, his hands running through my hair, trying to get purchase to hold on.

Maybe I ought to grow my hair out a little.

We didn't have anything to use for what I really wanted. Apparently Linden took lube to forests, but not gardens. Too bad, but when I glanced up at the long, slender, pale lines of his torso in the moonlight, it didn't matter. I'd fuck him later. I'd fuck him until he screamed, and when he whimpered and bit his lip I realized I'd said that out loud.

I left the stockings on when I took the underwear off him, propping his silk-clad thighs over my shoulders. I'd take them off later. Slowly.

My cock had to stay out of the game for the moment, but I did everything else, with my lips and tongue and fingers, around him and inside him, as he pushed back against me and spread his legs and clawed at the grass.

"Callum, please, please, oh, what are you doing—"

He broke off in a wail as I speared my tongue into him as deep as I could, and then he came all over my hand and his own belly, ropes of glistening white.

I licked it all up before I made my way back up to his mouth. Linden shuddered under me with every swipe of my tongue, making little sounds of pleasure that I wished I could swallow down the way I could swallow this part of him.

I'd meant this to be for him, but when he snaked a hand down and pulled my cock out of my pants, I couldn't stop him. He wrapped his hand around me and stroked me hard, and I came leaning down over him, my face pressed against his neck, every muscle clenching.

When we finally curled up together on the grass, catching our breath, I smiled up at the fading stars. The moon had finally set, and pre-dawn gray had seeped in to replace it. Linden snuggled against my side, tucking his head under my chin.

No sorcerers hunting us. No battle to come, no hostages, no fear.

I held him a little tighter, remembering that night in the forest. I didn't need to let him go this time.

I'd kept him safe.

Now I got to keep *him*.

His arm wrapped over my waist felt a little rigid, like he wanted to make sure of it.

Oskar had asked me what my intentions were, and I hadn't answered him. I hadn't been able to.

Now I thought I could, even though Linden hadn't asked. He shouldn't have to, after all.

"I'm never going anywhere," I said, answering the tension in his hold on me rather than the question he maybe didn't have the courage to ask. "Not without you. I'm not letting you out of my sight, and the next fucking awful party we have to go to, I'll be standing right behind you the whole time. Or next to you. Wherever bodyguards are supposed to stand at fancy parties in this realm."

His arm relaxed, and he started to pet me. Better, much

better.

"I heard a joke in the human realm," Linden said into my chest. "Something about a very large gorilla sitting wherever it wanted to. I think maybe you get to stand wherever you want at fancy parties. Who's going to dare to stop you?"

That startled a laugh out of me, jouncing his head on my chest. He poked me in the side, and I caught his hand and brought it up to my lips, carefully kissing each of his fingertips before I laid it back on my stomach, holding it wrapped in mine.

"As long as you want me there, I can live with terrifying everyone. At least no one else'll try to grope you. Fucker. He's lucky I didn't snap his neck."

Linden lifted his head, his lips quirking in amusement, a mischievous light in his eyes. "I could have gotten rid of him myself," he admitted.

I stared at him. That little...I'd known he was playing me.

Linden started to laugh, collapsing onto my chest in helpless giggles. I flipped him, rolling on top and making him gasp.

As I gazed down at him, not sure how I'd gotten so fucking lucky, he smiled up at me. A real smile, carefree and joyful.

Gray dawn gave way to rose and gold, and as I looked at him in wonder, the sun came up.

The End

For more action, adventure, snark, and steam, check out *The Alpha's Warlock*...

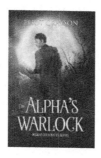

Cursed, mated, and in for the fight of their lives...

Warlock Nate Hawthorne just wants a cup of coffee. Is that too much to ask? Apparently. Because instead of precious caffeine, all he gets is cursed by a pack of werewolves who want to use him for his magic. Now the only way to fix the damage is a mate bond to a grumpy and oh-so-sexy alpha in the rival pack, who happens to hate him. This is so not how he wanted to start his day.

Ian Armitage never intended to take Nate as his mate. The Hawthorne family *can't* be trusted. Ian knows that better than anyone. The fact that he's lusted after the way-too-gorgeous man for years? Totally irrelevant. Ian's just doing what is necessary to protect his pack. This whole mating arrangement has nothing to do with love and never will. That's his story and he's sticking to it.

Nate and Ian will have to work together if they have any hope of staving off the pack's enemies and averting disaster. That's assuming they can stop arguing (and keep their hands off each other) long enough to save the day...

The Alpha's Warlock is an explicit M/M paranormal romance featuring a snarky warlock, a brooding alpha werewolf, knotting, enchanted socks (long story), and a guaranteed happily ever after.

Acknowledgments

My thanks as always go to my readers, especially the readers in my lovely Facebook group, for their encouragement along the way. I appreciate you very much!

Particular thanks are due to Alessandra Hazard and Amy Pittel for their invaluable beta reading, and for consistently calling out my errors and derp moments. Both of them should be held blameless for anything wrong with this book. Believe me, they did their best!

Additional thanks to Meghan Maslow for inviting me to write a book in the Magic Emporium series, and to the other authors involved in the project for being so much damn fun to work with. I had a blast. While that multi-author series has now been broken up by mutual agreement so that we could all use our books to launch series of our own, I'm couldn't be more honored to have had my name associated with all of my fellow authors on the project!

Get in Touch

I love hearing from readers! Find me at eliotgrayson.com, where I'll periodically post information about upcoming releases, including excerpts, or on Amazon, where you can find my other books. You can also sign up for my newsletter for occasional updates about what I'm writing or publishing next, or join my Facebook group, Eliot Grayson's Escape from Reality. Thanks for reading!

Also by Eliot Grayson

Mismatched Mates
The Alpha's Warlock
Captive Mate
A Very Armitage Christmas
The Alpha Experiment
Lost and Bound
Lost Touch
The Alpha Contract
The Alpha's Gamble

Blood Bonds
First Blood
Twice Bitten

Santa Rafaela
The One Decent Thing
A Totally Platonic Thing
Need a Hand?

Goddess-Blessed
The Replacement Husband
The Reluctant Husband
Yuletide Treasure

Portsmouth
Like a Gentleman
Once a Gentleman

Deven and the Dragon

Undercover

The Wrong Rake

Made in the USA
Monee, IL
31 January 2025

10379547R00111